Tomboy

Looking on the Heart Book 2

Books by Heather M. Green
Coming Home

Looking on the Heart Series
Fan Girl

Caged Heart Series
Matters of the Heart
The Heart of the Matter
Caging Her Heart

Red Rock Romance Series
Love, Lily
My Best Friend

Tomboy

Looking on the Heart Book 2

Heather M. Green

Cover Photo created by souvenirpixels
Cover Design by Heather M. Green

3

For
Tate & Sheri

Acknowledgments

Thanks to my proof/beta readers: Jamie Coy, Chelsey Hickenlooper, Amanda Lamb, Paula Maddock, Ashley DeFreitas, Courtney Lamb, and Hadlee Bingham

Tomboy (N)- a girl who enjoys rough, noisy activities usually associated with boys

Unctuous (Adj)- excessively or ingratiatingly flattering

Charlatan (N)- a fraud

Placid (Adj)- calm, peaceful, quiet, undisturbed

Ambiguous (Adj)- unclear or confusing

Opaque (Adj)- Not able to be seen through; not transparent

Nomenclature (N)- the body or system of names in a particular field

Pariah (N)- an outcast

Wraith (N)- a ghost or ghostlike image of someone, especially one seen shortly before or after their death

Palter (V)- to talk or act insincerely or deceitfully

Dissemble (V)- to hide under a false appearance

Prologue

I stared down the dusty road, straining my eyes for one more glimpse of him before the curtain of swirling dust or the bend in the red, gritty road took him from me forever. Without a downward glance, I swatted at the deer fly unfortunate enough to land on my forearm, angrily taking my disappointment and broken heart out on the greedy insect. Funny that the bite should even register in my brain since I hadn't noticed them in weeks. My stinging smack shouldn't have undone me. I'm stronger than that. I prove it everyday living in the shadow of my perfect sister. But the violent act gave me a good, if not juvenile, reason to allow the tears that were pooling in my forgettable hazel eyes to slip silently down my sun-kissed cheeks.

I had known from the moment I saw him that we'd never be, but young love is stupid, hopeful and gluttonous. As impulsive as it is clueless.

I'd once asked Brant how he made friends so easily. I don't. But I'd been willing to change. In situations like these, it's too bad I was the smart one all along. If I hadn't allowed myself to be his friend, I wouldn't be hurting now.

Life has a way of forcing unwanted education on you. There's no escaping the hollow emptiness that comes with painful wisdom gained. Maybe I'd look back one day and appreciate the time we'd had together regardless of the outcome.

But today...I'd cry.

Chapter 1

I stepped from the car, lifting my sunglasses to the top of my head. The blazing sun blinded me, making me squint. I immediately rethought my decision and lowered the glasses back down over my hazel eyes.

Boring hazel eyes.

I wondered once again why I had to get hazel when my older brother had piercing baby blues and my younger sister had velvety chocolate brown.

I used the black elastic around my wrist to pull my plain brown hair up into a messy bun and shouldered my dark purple duffle bag. Tucking my pillow with the navy case and glow-in-the-dark constellations print under my arm, I trudged across the dry, red dirt and gravel to the cabin. A persistent deer fly hitched a ride on my bare arm and I huffed a breath at it, trying unsuccessfully to get it to move on.

Opening the rickety screen door, I took a deep breath of familiar cabin air that was one part sagebrush and two parts musty disuse, and smiled. I'd have to air it out later which meant hours of cleaning, but I didn't care. A small price to pay for the rewards of a summer of solitude at the lake.

Finally. My summer home. My reason for existing the other nine months of the year.

We'd been coming to our family's cabin since before I could remember. And although it isn't as spectacular as some of the other cabins nearby, it's ours. My second home. My *favorite* home; the home I go to in my mind during Utah's freezing winter months, wet springs, and colorful autumns. These three scorching summer months make the remaining months worth living. Just me, my poetry, and the lake. Especially the lake. It's crisp and clear. Pine and aspen stand shoulder to shoulder on three sides in a combined effort to keep it shady during the day in all the right places. It turns down the outside temperature to simmering- bearable.

Some call it quiet, secluded. Take for instance, the seasoned woman whose wrinkles attested to the world that she'd earned the right to take a dip in nothing but what the good Lord gave her. I still smile about the moment of panic summers ago when Dad had fumbled to shield our eyes but wasn't completely thorough because his own eyes were closed, while Mom had taken the 'free spirit' a much-needed towel. But we'd seen enough. Our family trip to the lake that year had turned more educational than my parents bargained for. I mean it was summer break, after all.

That was years ago. That good old gal has probably moved on by now, hopefully personally conversing with the Lord in more than she had on that day. Because...awkward. But the lake is still here.

Some call it restful. Like the year we stumbled over- quite literally- a couple unfortunate enough to fall asleep in the tall grasses off one side of the glassy lake, a few yards from the water's edge. I don't know how long they'd been there, but I didn't envy their half-baked, lobster-red state. And I'd been close enough to get a lasting mental image of that lovely shade, what with being right on top of them. That had to hurt! I know my sprained wrist did.

Hope they felt a particular attachment to the bathing suits they wore because that's probably about all they could stand to wear for weeks after.

I personally felt they could have shown a little more gratitude for our scaring years off their life in the name of getting out of the sun. But we were just pesky kids. What did we know?

The couple is happily married to this day. We wave and covertly laugh/cringe behind our hands when we see them at the cabin down the road. I'm sure they've discovered sunblock.

The sunburns and sprained wrist are gone. But the lake is still here.

Some call it adventurous. But only if you aren't Bailey, my sister. She hasn't forgiven our brother, Brant, or me for pulling the *Parent Trap* `a la lake* move. I mean she went completely under! Just dropped out of sight.

At least that's how I pieced it together from the facts spit at me by Bailey- along with a little lake water- and the snorted retelling from Brant.

We didn't see any harm done. I'm the one who almost drowned when Brant forgot he was standing on my shoulders because he was laughing so hard. But I felt vindicated when he lost his balance and slapped down on the water like a wooden soldier face-planting hard. Talk about your epic belly flops!

Ironically enough, he came up just like Bailey-coughing and sputtering. But unlike Bailey, he sported a nice red welt on his chest for twenty minutes after.

It was a harmless prank. She knows how to swim. All's well that ends well. She's just angry because it messed up her perfect hair.

Years later, her hair is still annoyingly perfect and Brant's welt is long gone. But the lake is still here.

In my brain, each year is divided into locations, not months: the city months and the lake months.

My family had packed coolers, totes, and kayaks for our stay. It had been almost a year since we'd been here and I couldn't wait to jump into my swimming suit and dip my feet into the glassy blue lake a quarter mile down the windy dirt road.

I raced quickly up the stairs to the loft to claim my twin bed in the far corner of the room. Even the knowledge that I'd be stuck sharing this space with my sister for the foreseeable future couldn't wipe the smile from my face or the peace from my heart that had taken up residence the moment we traded paved road for dirt, and city smog for more breathable, less chewable mountain air.

With my sleeping bag set out until we washed sheets to make up the twin beds, I stripped down to my undies and pulled my tankini from my bag. I studied it with turned down lips. The suit had been teal with small, multi-colored flowers when I bought it, but all the time spent lazing on the dock in the sun last summer had faded it to a pale blue with unrecognizable blobs. The top was a little tight this year, I noticed as I tugged it down, and then shimmied and resituated because I looked more like a girl finally. But no matter how much cleavage I managed to gain over the past twelve months, I was still the lanky, mousy girl my brother's friends teased about being 'just one of the guys'.

Get over it, Charlie. But my attempt at positive self-talk only reaffirmed how much I really was one of the boys, right down to my name. I shrugged, grateful for the lack of a mirror to point out my late bloomer status and swiped my notebook and towel from my sleeping area. I slipped into my flip flops and bounced down the stairs.

"I'm walking to the lake," I announced, throwing my towel over my shoulder.

Brantley, side-swiped me as he shouldered past with a sloshing water jug. "Mom wants you to bring in one of the coolers and load the food into the fridge."

"Ugh," I moaned. "You sure she didn't ask you and you're trying to get out of it?"

My brother smirked. "Would I do that?"

"I'm not even going to answer."

"She really told me to ask you to help," he insisted.

I dropped my towel and notebook on the lodgepole pine couch. "Fine."

"Hurry and I'll race you to the lake."

I hopped down the steps and out to our ancient SUV and hefted the cooler from the back. Shuffling to the cabin under the weight of a couple weeks worth of food and seeing Bailey through the screen door, I banged on the creaky wood casing with one foot.

My sister, Bailey-the-beautiful, shoved the door open, knocking it into the cooler and bumping me backward. "You could put the cooler down and open the door yourself, Charles," she huffed then grinned wickedly. I hated when she called me that. "Or did that not occur to you?"

I squeezed past her, turning the cooler sideways so it would fit through the doorway. "You could help us carry stuff in," I grouched back. "But of course, that would never occur to you."

"Mom told you and Brant to do it." She flipped her blonde hair over her shoulder and flounced to the stairs leading to the loft. "You better not have taken my corner," she hollered over her shoulder.

"It's not *your* corner. And don't touch my stuff!" I closed my eyes and made a list of synonyms for 'entitled' in my mind. Chasing after her would only make it worse. Instead, I continued on to the kitchen to unload the cooler.

"Why are *you* emptying the cooler?" Mom asked, coming into the cabin. "I told Bailey to do it."

Apparently the message was lost in transit like that telephone game we used to play at birthday parties when I was five. I shrugged. "It's okay. I don't mind helping." I grinned slyly. "As long as I get to stay at the lake until dinner."

She brushed past me and planted a kiss on the side of my head- as high as her vertically challenged lips could reach. And that was on tiptoe. "I'll do you one better than that," she said. "I'll get Bailey to help cook dinner tonight. The deep cleaning can wait until tomorrow morning. You enjoy the lake. We'll save you a plate."

"Really?" My eyes rounded in surprised delight. "Thanks, Mom." I quickly shelved milk and eggs and slammed the fridge door.

"Brantley!" I hollered as I swiped my towel off the couch and made a beeline for the front door, not caring that the door banged shut behind me or that my mother's predictable, "Hey! Don't let the screen door slam!" followed. I clomped down the wooden steps and filled my lungs with woodsy air. "Let's go."

Unctuous

You stand tall and inviting.
Broad. Safe. Full of life.
Solid arms fan out and up. Reaching. Shading my place of
contemplation.
Like an old friend, you wait patiently, at the edge of the dock to
welcome me.
I run to you and collapse against your strength. Happiness.
Relief.
Gnarled legs spread out and down. Searching. Entangling me
in a reprieve.
Rough. Grasping. Drained of life.
You stand tall and inviting.
                                        -The Skinny Tomboy

•••••

"Chaaarles!"

My pen skuddled over the paper and dragged an angry line across the page.

Ugh.

With a finger in the notebook to mark my place I closed the cover and gave my sister a tight smile.

"What's up?"

"Your hair," Bailey laughed and pointed.

I reached a hand up to smooth my semi-dry hair, cringing when I encountered what must have looked like a matted rat's nest perched on top of my head. The lake was doing me no favors today.

"Thank you," I said curtly.

"I don't know how you can even get in that disgusting water. Fish." She shuddered. "The fish poop. Who knows what's in there. Not to mention it's freezing!"

With a sigh, I set my notebook on the dock and ran my fingers through my tangled hair, pulling it into a ponytail.

"Then I'm surprised you're down here. The walk alone..." My voice trailed off.

"I know. The stupid road messes up my pedicure." She pointed a sandaled foot and studied her polished toes, now coated in a thin layer of brown-red dust. "Hm. Pedicures." She gave me a sweeping glance, lingering at my feet.

I refused to hide them, though I squirmed inside.

"What do you want, Bailey?" I demanded.

"Mom said it's your night to help with dinner." When I didn't move, she said, "You need to come now."

Our eyes locked in a silent face-off. Her fists clenched and a smile tugged at my lips. She was fifteen going on twenty-four, but I'd only give her so much power over me today. I was in my sanctuary after a long dry spell and no one, least of all my diva little sister, was going to spoil it for me.

With a huff of exasperated breath, she turned and pranced up the dock. "Sorry about your bed," she called without a backward glance.

I closed my eyes against the anger trying to creep in. I knew I wouldn't like what awaited me in the loft just as I knew her 'sorry' was a joke about as funny as the fact that she patronized me by bothering with the reconciliatory word. The question now was: Anger or no anger? Revenge then?

I leaned back on one hand, letting the other hand search for the lake lapping eagerly at the edge of the dock. When the cool water tickled my fingers, I felt the anger drain through my fingertips, and the lake took it from me.

I picked up my notebook- my one prized possession- and turned to the next page- a clean sheet full of possibilities.

A Gift
Wrapped in nature's perfect package.
Clear.
Cool.
Soothing.
Placid.
Lapping.
Rough.
Irritating.
Stifling.
Ambiguous.
Wrapped in nature's perfect package.
　　　　　　　　　　　　-The Skinny Tomboy

"Sorry to bother you," a male voice interrupted.

I looked up from my notebook with a sigh. Why couldn't everyone just leave me alone?

"Your family owns a cabin a few down from mine," the guy said, shifting his weight from one foot to the other.

"Uh, yeah," I replied. "You look a little familiar." He looked to be in his early to mid twenties. While some may consider him good looking, he had an unkempt way about him that made me uncomfortable.

The guy smiled, making him better looking and yet more creepy at the same time. "You've seen me then?"

I wanted to squirm. "Um, just in passing, I think." I'd maybe seen him on the porch of his parent's cabin a time or two over the years. What did he want anyway?

"But you remembered me," he pressed.

"Maybe." My voice was noncommittal. I was definitely starting to get a creeper vibe from this guy.

"My name's Josh."

"Hello," I said. No way was I telling him my name.

He noticed, but only smiled. "You guys come here every summer, right?"

"Yes." I stood, clutching my towel and notebook to my chest. "I need to go."

"Too bad," he said, eyeing me from the tip of my plain brown hair down to my unpainted toenails. "I'll see you around."

Hopefully not. I hurried past him without a reply, cringing when I felt his eyes follow me. I wanted to hurry away faster, but was afraid my butt would jiggle if I did and I didn't want him looking. My swimming suit wasn't revealing, but I would have felt naked in a burka around that guy.

Chapter 2

"Sometimes I wish we had a dog," I confided in Brant the next day as I spread my arms wide and glided like a really ungraceful figure skater across the foamy rug we set out on the small patch of lawn behind the cabin.

Brant had been saddled this year with the task of washing the rugs that padded the cabin floors. Every summer we ask why we can't just throw them into the washing machine, and every year Mom insists they be hand washed. Who knows…I think it goes back to her young years of forced child labor with Great Depression-Era grandparents.

So what do kids do when they don't want to do the assigned chore? We made a game of it. Instead of being down on hands and knees with a bar of soap and scrub brush- boring and so twentieth century- we brush up on our artistic talents with liquid dish soap skillfully applied in creative patterns over the rugs and then use our feet as the scrub brush.

If you don't think of it as work, it's actually therapeutic in a warped way. And we usually end up more wet than the rugs do.

Today would be no exception, it seemed.

"Whoooa!" I let out a startled squeal as I hit a non-soapy patch of rug and pitched forward, arms flailing. With a very dignified 'oof' I landed in the suds on my stomach like an anorexic seal on a slip-n-slide.

I stood with a dramatic bow for Brant's benefit and ended up with a face full of water.

"Agggh. Brant! What are you doing?"

"You were covered in soap," he explained with an innocent shrug. But his exploding grin and the spewing hose told the real story.

"Thanks for the rinse," I replied wryly.

I watched as Brant rinsed the rug and hung it over the deck railing to dry in the afternoon sun. I turned the hose off and took a seat in one of the Adirondack chairs lining the deck. Brant leaned casually against the railing, watching me.

"A dog, huh? Why only sometimes?"

"I don't know. I think it would be nice to have someone to confide in who never voices their opinion. They just listen without judgment."

"Who's judging?" he asked, spreading his arms wide and looking around.

When I was slow to answer, he prodded. "Come on, Charlie. You can tell me. This is a judgment free zone." His hands moved in a circular motion, including the small area surrounding us. "You're safe here."

I looked up at his practiced clinical voice and giggled. "Yeah. I felt so safe when I was being drowned a few minutes ago."

He grinned. "That wasn't the safe zone. Let's go over this one more time." He drew a circle in the air with his finger encompassing me and the chairs. "Safe zone." Then he pointed two feet away. "Not-safe zone."

My eyes narrowed. "It's difficult to see the distinction."

"Not to the practiced eye."

"I think your 'safe zone' boundaries blur from time to time."

"It's possible," he admitted. "Whatever suits my purposes."

I snorted. "That's what I figured. You are slightly diabolical and distrubed."

"Yes. I've been told that."

"So, the dog…" I said, getting him back on track.

"I've thought of bringing up the subject with Mom and Dad before."

"So why didn't you? It would give you something to do while we're here all summer." I studied him. "I know this isn't your favorite place."

He peered at me closely. "But it is yours."

I nodded solemnly. "Yes. And I know you'd rather go somewhere else every summer, but you agree for my sake." I tapped my index finger on the arm of the chair. "Thank you," I said softly, staring a hole in the thigh of my shorts.

Brant shifted uncomfortably, crossing and uncrossing his arms. "I'm not sure what you're talking about."

"Fine. We won't talk about how you fought for the cabin for me instead of the road trip Dad wanted to take." Brant was selfless like that when it came to me. But I didn't always feel good about getting my way. Especially when I knew that Brant would have loved the road trip as much as Dad. And for a lot of reasons, probably, Brant would never admit he did it for me.

More shifting and lots of deafening silence.

"You love a good road trip," I accused without malice.

"You heard that conversation?"

I stood and walked to the railing, leaning more against Brant than the wooden post. "We aren't talking about it. Remember?" I reached up and kissed his cheek. "You are my favorite sibling," I said over his disgusted protests.

"Oh, go write poetry or something," he answered with a gentle shove.

"You can't stop me from loving you, Brant," I called over my shoulder as I made my way inside the cabin.

"If you love me so much," he called after me, "don't skip out on helping me with the last two rugs."

"Do you want me to write poetry- meaning leave you alone- or do you want me to clean rugs?" I returned.

"Are you going to get all mushy on me?" he asked.

"Probably," I replied with a saucy smile.

"Definitely write poetry." He waved me away with his hand.

•••••

"That's the last of the towels to go in," I reported, wiping my forehead with the back of my hand and stepping from the laundry room off the kitchen. It was a construction add-on when I was a little girl and I'm grateful for it. I think I would throw tantrums like Bailey if we had to hand wash all the towels and linens like we hand washed the rugs.

"Good," my mom replied in something more like a sigh than the actual word. "Thanks." She also wiped her forehead, but with her shoulder instead of her hand, and went back to kneading the dough for her homemade cinnamon rolls. The cool breeze of the morning had moved into the dry heat of afternoon and we were both feeling it. Not surprisingly, the lake was calling my name.

"And the windows are washed, the rugs are clean, and Bailey is nearly finished color coordinating her bottles of nail polish."

I snickered when Mom rolled her eyes. "Don't ask me," I said with a shrug. "I'm just reporting progress."

"How much dish soap do I still have?" she asked with a raised brow and a smirk.

"Um, marginally less than you started with?"

With a soft snort she went back to kneading. "What are your plans for today?" she asked. "Besides cleaning up after your sister." She frowned. "Did she damage your stuff too badly? I don't understand why she acts the way she does."

What? Like a spoiled brat? I wanted to ask. Instead, I shrugged, giving silent permission for her to stop blaming herself for my sister's immature behavior. "Nope. It's already cleaned up. No worries." I leaned over the mixing bowl and sniffed the dough appreciatively. "You should make these more often," I said, practically salivating. I gave her a peck on the cheek. "You're the best," I told her. "I'm headed to the lake, if that's okay with you."

"Yes. Have fun."

"I will." I paused at the bottom of the stairs. "And Mom...I'm a big girl. Don't worry about Bailey." I jogged partway up the stairs, then stopped. "I was thinking," I called down to her. "Next year maybe we should only stay here half the time." I shrugged. "You know. Try someplace new. Maybe Brant has a suggestion."

Invisible
Contradicting. Superiority. Contempt. Disdain. Contention.
For one so invisible, I feel naked and exposed.
My champion cheers from the shadows.
Invisible to all but me.
     -The Skinny Tomboy

•••••

"Remember Kristin and Matt are coming Friday morning," Mom said one morning two weeks later.

I glanced up from my bowl of fruit, yogurt and granola as she passed through the kitchen to the laundry room. "I remember," I replied around a plump raspberry.

"They are bringing their son. You need to be nice and actually talk to him."

I swallowed. Ugh.

But Mom knows I needed time to work up to these things. Socializing isn't my strongest point. I don't have very many people I call friends. There is...well, there was...Ok. I can count on zero hands the number of friends I have. I have *acquaintances* at school- people I talk to for group projects or offering apologies when I stumble into them in the halls because I'm focused on my latest read or poem.

"I'll try," I promised, hopping off the bar stool and taking my bowl to the sink. Say hi? Of course. I could be polite. More than that? All I could offer was that I'd try. For her. But carrying on an extended conversation day after day or entertaining some dirty, post elementary kid for the next two weeks? Not a chance. I was used to babysitting for people in the neighborhood on an occasional Friday night, but this? This was too much. I couldn't talk and hang out with kids my own age, let alone someone younger. And in *my* sanctuary! What would we talk about? I didn't even know the first thing about Spiderman or Captain Hulk and his Marvel cronies.

I snatched up my towel and notebook off the island.

"Have you seen your sister?" she called from behind a full laundry basket.

"I think she said something about going into town with Brant." I stopped with a hand on the screen door. "I'll be at the lake if you need me."

"Will you be home for lunch?" she asked.

"I have an apple," I assured her.

"I'll see you when I see you," she said with a knowing smile and a slight shake of her head.

"Love you."

A party of one

I am people.

I am me.

I am simple solitude.

People passing like cars on a highway. With a purpose that doesn't involve people. Here one second and out of range the next. But I don't mind. My purpose doesn't involve people either.

I am simple solitude.

I am me.

I am people.

-The Skinny Tomboy

I rolled onto my back and stared through the lacy patchwork of leaves far above me. The sun struggled to reach me as a slight breeze blew leaves across its path, making it zig and zag around them to land on my cheeks and forehead- a strange sensation of being chilled everywhere but my face.

This was the life!

I stored my pen in my notebook and stood, taking my towel with me. I gave it one good shake to leave the dirt and dried leaves behind and walked to the water's edge where my turquoise kayak waited. I tossed my notebook into the storage compartment and spread my towel over the seat.

As I dug my paddle into the water, a noise behind me on the dock had me glancing back. Josh. That guy from the other day. My heart rate spiked and the day didn't seem so perfect anymore. He grinned and offered a small wave. I ducked my head and paddled away as fast as I could.

Twenty minutes later, I rested my paddle across my lap. My shoulder muscles and triceps were tight with exertion and I wished I'd remembered to bring a water bottle with me. I raised a hand to shield my eyes from the bright sun and looked around me.

A hawk drifted in lazy circles on an invisible aircurrent overhead. I looked for its reflection on the water's surface, but couldn't see it. Its shrill scream was drowned out by an adrenaline filled cry that echoed off the canyon walls, followed by a satisfying splash as someone conquered their fear and charged off a perfectly good cliff into nothingness, hanging suspended briefly before falling forty feet through the air to the clear water below.

I would never understand why people took risks like that. Life is too beautiful to throw away on super-charged, thoughtless stunts done on a dare. Still, I picked up my paddle and dug into the water to make my way to the popular jumping spot.

I arrived in time to see Brant leap into the air without a second thought. Arms and legs flailing, he gave a warrior call of triumph as he plunged through the air and into the water.

I watched until he surfaced with his fist in the air. The kids standing high on the cliff above him cheered. He pumped his fist in the air again.

I smiled at his enthusiasm, his carefree spirit and way of approaching life. Apparently he traded in the idea of a dog for finding people to hang with.

Brant was like that- making friends easily, no matter where we went. Being with people was as effortless for him as breathing. He was happier when he was surrounded by crowds, laughing, talking, having what he considered to be a good time. He was quick-witted and loved to tease and joke. Life was exciting to him. He was always in search of the next adventure.

I frowned.

College. That was his next big adventure. I knew he was dying to go. But we didn't talk about it.

I *wouldn't* talk about it.

As soon as the summer wavered between warm and cool, he'd be gone. At nearly nineteen, he was ready to take on the world.

That was Brant.

That wasn't me.

When I graduated after this coming school year, I didn't know where I'd go. Or *if* I'd go.

I watched in awe as Brant scaled the rocky cliff to join his newly acquired friends for another dive. A weight settled in my chest and I dug my paddle in, focusing on a different canyon. Maybe I'd spend next summer here by myself. Figure myself out.

Maybe.

Chapter 3

"You remember the Stewarts are coming tonight," Mom asked over our early breakfast together. Just the two of us on the deck in our hoodies, enjoying the crisp morning and a multigrain bagel with strawberry cream cheese. Nice.

Brant and Dad had gone hiking up one of the canyons the night before and were expected to be back tonight. "Before the Stewarts arrive," Mom had told Dad with that 'mom' look. He'd promised they'd be back.

And Bailey was getting her beauty sleep. I gave an inward eye roll. Wish it could work for her attitude as well. Her insides could use a little beauty.

"Yes, Mom. How could I forget?" She'd only reminded me almost daily for three weeks.

"I should really be reminding Bailey, I guess," she said with a sigh bordering on discouragement. "I don't need to tell you she doesn't play nice with others very often."

"She plays nice," I disagreed.

Mom's brows rose in surprise at my compliment, but quickly fell when I added, "When she gets her way."

"I know. How did I raise three very different children?"

"Lucky, I guess," I responded.

"I worry for Kristin's son if he's cute."

My brows pulled together. Why would it matter to Bailey if some little tween kid was cute? She wouldn't give him a second glance. She prided herself on getting and holding the attention of older guys. And because she looked and acted old for her age, she usually got what she wanted in that department. "She'll play with him like a puppy for a day or two, if she pays any attention to him at all, and then kick him into the lake."

Mom's lips twitched. "That's what I'm worried about." But then her voice was stern with a reprimand. "Be nice, Charlie. She's the only sister you have."

"Lucky me," I muttered. That's a reminder I *really* didn't need.

•••••

"They're here!"

My mom's excited cry startled me from my own head. I glanced at her and then out the window for clues about who these people were that were about to invade my sanctuary for the next two weeks.

I recognized Kristin. I'd seen her before in old pictures or yearbooks Mom occasionally pulled out when she was feeling nostalgic. Although the pictures were ridiculous in a nineties-big-hair kind of way, she was pretty. Even now, she was beautiful for someone her age. Her dark hair was thick and pulled up in a messy bun. She was stylish in a 'mom' sort of way and I found it easy to match her to faded pictures of a younger, more giggly version of this adult woman. Though the laughing-so-hard-we-literally-peed-our-pants image from Mom's numerous stories over the years? I couldn't see it.

Kristin's husband was a big guy. Tall, but not gangly like me. Broad through the shoulders with a little bit of a Dad Bod going on. The slight paunch would have been more pronounced had he been shorter. Laugh lines bordered their eyes and smiles like quotation marks on life well lived.

They looked like people I could get along with.

And then...I saw their son.

I blinked, inhaled a sharp breath of surprise and unceremoniously choked on my spit.

"You okay, Charlie?" Dad asked as he headed to answer the door. But Mom hurried past him and swung the door open with an excited squeal.

I didn't respond to Dad's question. I couldn't.

My mom and I have a pretty great relationship. She's funny and not uptight. She works like a slave for us, and I honest to goodness appreciate her. And if Bailey was anything to go by, we get along way better than most girls my age and their mothers. But at this moment, I wanted to yell at her that she'd tricked me. I wanted to be crazy angry with her for blindsiding me.

How could she let me believe the Stewart's son was some eleven or twelve year old awkward tween with braces, stubborn baby fat, and an unruly cowlick or something? The reality was vastly different.

I figured he was probably about Brant's age. And trust me when I say this *man* was not awkward in any way. No braces in sight. Clunky clown feet that didn't fit his body yet? Pre-adolescent pimples? Hardly. They wouldn't dare.

He was as tall as his dad, but not as broad through the shoulders. Time, I shivered to imagine, would fix that for him. No dad bod for...

What was his name again? Arthur? Abel? Why couldn't I think?

"*Axyl*," Bailey practically purred from her perch at the window like she read my mind. A scary thought.

Almost as scary as my next thought.

While I cringed at Bailey's outward expression of obvious instant infatuation, and Brant muttered a soft 'uh-oh,' I wanted to throw up because for once in my life, she and I agreed on something.

This was bad. Really bad. And it was *his* fault. Why couldn't he be a homely tween still clinging to that unfair extra layer of fat that mysteriously disappears as soon as your height decides to catch up with the rest of your disproportionate body parts? You know...awkward. But there was nothing awkward about him. At least visually. He was beautiful!

Sadly, I knew his type. I lived with it every day of my life. He was a male version of Bailey.

He had simultaneously become the enemy and the curiosity...er obsession? I gave a mental head shake. No, curiosity. Curiosity.

Axyl.

I tried his name out, silently rolling it around on my tongue. It was two parts forbidden bad boy and one part intriguing male. I was disturbed to find it felt exciting in my mouth. Like stumbling upon arresting, evocative poetry from an unknown artist that takes you somewhere you've never been before and moves you to tears. An unexpected treasure that you secretly want to keep to yourself because you are changed eternally. And you welcome the change. It is new, exhilarating, and freeing.

I was seriously fangirling here and it was beginning to freak me out. This wasn't me- tempted by an untouchable, pretty face. I know when they are too far out of my league to even dabble in the formulation of the thought. I don't write stupid, sappy love poetry. I've never been one of the silly, giggly girls who look at guys and *see* them. I don't look at guys. Period.

Agggh. The thought makes me sick. It's like I'm not even myself anymore.

I take a deep breath and close my eyes to center myself. I'm level-headed. I have this enormous vocabulary that is suddenly reduced to sputtering words like cute and cuddly. It's like falling from the paradise of the lake back down to the smelly city. I've fallen from grace. I'm an idiot.

I'm an idiot!

People like him don't look twice at people like me.

Bailey? Maybe.

Probably.

Who was I kidding? They'll practically be married when the fourteen days are up. Forget that he's legal and she's not. Forget that he's probably headed for college at the end of the summer like Brant and she's just starting high school. Forget everything you've ever known about the way life should work because Bailey gets what Bailey wants.

Always.

Without question.

I pulled myself from my thoughts in time to watch Mom and Kristin gush and hug each other and Matt and Dad shake hands and do the man hug thing. Then I watched as Brant approached Axyl with a large grin. Axyl held up a fist and Brant bumped it like they were long lost friends.

I tell you. So, so Brant. Instant friends with everyone.

And then there was Bailey. Ugh. My eyes can't roll hard enough. I shuddered at the predatory smile on her face and sent a screaming mental message to Axyl to turn and run far and fast.

She held out a hand for Axyl to take and let it linger a few seconds too long. What is this, the nineteenth century? If she wasn't obvious, I don't know what in this world is. Add to that the mega-flirtatious smile through her lashes and the coy way she said, "Axyl. I'm Bailey," and no one had any doubts she was staking her claim on this guy for the next two weeks and far into the future.

She giggled at something he said and batted at his arm in a flirty way. I didn't miss the victorious smile she threw at me. Nor did I care.

"Finally someone around here interesting enough to hang with," Bailey cooed, letting her hand slip down his arm to his hand. Again with the smug look in my direction. "You are going to love the lake. Let's change and I'll walk you down there."

Put a reign on her, Mom. Please. I silently begged. *Before she embarrasses us all.*

That screaming mental message reached its intended target because my mom grabbed Bailey's arm and pulled her in next to her side real tight. "They need to unpack, Bailey," my mom muttered. Bailey growled under her breath, but she stayed put. Thank heaven.

But the embarrassment was just beginning. It was my turn for introductions.

"Oh, Charlie," Kristin cried, beaming at me. "Look how grown up she is, Matt." She put a hand on her husband's arm. "Remember that night- I don't want to even think about how many years ago it was- we were together playing card games at your house, Mindy, and Charlie was getting out of the bathtub? How old was she- three?" Kristin and my mother started to laugh and my face flamed bright. I didn't know this story, but I instantly dreaded whatever was coming next in their little walk down memory lane.

"You came out of the bathroom in a huge towel," Mom picked up the story, "and said, 'Maaatt, look at meee.' You opened your towel and flashed us all."

Oh, could my life get any more mortifying at this moment? I could throw myself into the lake right now, not even on a dare, and not feel bad as the life drained from my body. I was that embarrassed. Brant's obnoxious laughter added to my misery because I knew I'd never hear the end of it from him. Like for the rest of my life.

Kristin immediately put a comforting arm around my shoulders. "Oh, Charlie," she uttered, "I'm so sorry. That wasn't very nice of me. I didn't mean to embarrass you. It was just so cute. We laughed about it for weeks." And years, apparently. They were obviously still laughing about it and had now included the next generation in my shame.

And in front of their too hot son.

And Brant.

And Bailey. Oh, gag. Bailey would be all over that story like flies on crap. As if she needed more ammo to fire at me.

Thank you very much Kristin Stewart.

Matt patted my shoulder. "Good to see you again, Charlie."

"And even better that it's fully clothed," Brant remarked.

My scathing look and my mother's warning, "Brant..." went unnoticed because he was bending over with laughter at his own joke.

And that's why I didn't see Axyl approach.

"Charlie," he said, standing directly in front of me, blocking me from Brant's laughter. Curiosity framed the way he said my name and I almost liked it. His appraising look felt nerve wracking and a bit invasive considering he'd just heard about the peep show from my toddler years, but probably only to me. "*You're* Charlie?" He chuckled and gave a slight shake of his head. My face flamed.

Correction. I didn't like the way he said my name. In fact, I hated it. And I hated him. Instantly.

I knew more had just been revealed to him about me than anyone wanted to know. I knew I wasn't much to look at, especially compared to my younger sister. I also knew my name fit me way better physically than I ever cared to think about. And I hated my mother a little bit more for the boy name. But to laugh at me out right? The only comfort I could take from this moment was the fact that I had him pegged as a female version of Bailey from the second I saw him. Could I call it, or what? I frowned. It felt like a hollow victory with me getting a participation trophy.

And just like he'd done with Brant, he held out a fist to me. This is my life. Fist bumps and mockings. No wonder I never look at boys. What a waste of time and space.

"Hey," I got out between clenched teeth before turning away. I didn't miss the glare my mother gave me at my cool reception and quick escape. But what did she want from me? Bailey's embarrassing welcome more than made up for my lack. I cringed again thinking about it.

And then my cringe deepened as I remembered my brief stint with indecent exposure- my nudy story revealed for all the world to hear. Ugh and double ugh!

I couldn't get to the lake fast enough.

"Nice to see you again, Mr. and Mrs. Stewart," I managed over my shoulder.

"Not too long, Charlie," my mom called after me. "Dinner will be ready in twenty."

I waved a hand to let her know I'd heard her and high tailed it down the road to my sanctuary from awkward meetings with high expectations and even more awkward sisters.

Humiliation
Red hot over an exposed body.
Revealed plainly for all to witness.
Jeering laughter simultaneously covers and filets.
Laying wide my exposure, gaping.
                    -The Skinny Tomboy

Chapter 4

"Mom's never going to let you go out in public in that suit," I told Bailey the next day, eyeing the skimpy fabric of her new black and fuschia bikini. She had the body to pull it off; as she was well aware. I looked like the towering, gangly pre-adolescent sister next to her. And she wasn't one to let that detail pass without numerous jabbing comments.

Bailey stuck her nose in the air with a sniff. "She can't say anything. I bought it with my own money."

"At least put something over it," I tried. She'd have sun touching areas previously unexposed to the light of day.

"If anyone should be hiding, it's you." She scrunched her perfect button nose in disgust while looking me up and down. "I can't believe you're okay with being seen in that thing. The butt is sagging." She continued to eye me critically and I knew I came up lacking. "At least you finally got something upstairs so the top looks marginally passable. I'm embarrassed for you."

That made two of us. But I was saving my money for something more lasting than a small piece of spandex fabric. Something that made a difference in not only myself, hopefully, but in a lot of other people. In children. I would be brave for once, stand out and make a difference on my trip with a group next summer to a Mexican orphanage.

"You wouldn't understand," I replied. "There's no one here to impress anyway."

"What about *Axyl*?" Bailey purred his name.

"What *about* Axyl?" I slipped my feet into my flip flops and grabbed my towel and notebook.

Bailey snorted with disdain. "If I have to spell it out for you, then it doesn't matter." She shook her head sadly as if my lack of knowledge on whatever subject she was trying to press was pitiful. "Stay out of my way," she commanded, brushing past me to the door. The Victoria Secret cloud surrounding her blew me backward. "Axyl has noticed me. Did you see how close he sat while we played games last night? He smells *mmmm*," she hummed and giggled.

I wasn't going to remind her that we'd all been squished around the table like sardines. I had practically been in Brant's lap all night. I had a permanent bruise on my side from his elbow. Maybe I'd suggest card tables tonight so we could breathe.

She could think what she wanted about Axyl or otherwise. She did anyway. And I only half-listened to her drone on.

"And I'm not going to sit around writing stupid poetry in a book for the next two weeks."

She pushed the door open with dramatic flair and crunched down the drive.

"Whatever Bailey," I muttered. "See ya."

•••••

A shadow slid over me and I glanced up from my notebook, shielding my eyes from the blinding sun with a hand. Expecting Bailey, I opened my mouth to ask where she'd been. She'd left the cabin in her 'swimming suit' before I did, but she wasn't at the lake. I would know because I'd been sitting on the dock for over an hour. But I closed my mouth when I saw it was only Brant and Axyl.

"Can we sit?" Axyl asked, pointing to the spot beside me on the dock.

I shrugged. "I don't own the dock," I replied, going back to my writing.

"Be nice, Charlie," Brant reprimanded as he plopped down at the dock's edge and let his feet dangle in the water. "You'll have to forgive my sister. She says she doesn't own the dock, but she doesn't really mean it."

I ignored them both and chewed on the end of my pen, searching for the perfect word to describe how I felt when people invaded my territory.

"So your family owns the dock?" Axyl asked, eyebrows arching high on his forehead in surprise.

"No," Brant told him. "But the lake is Charlie's favorite place on Earth, and she doesn't like to be disturbed. Don't take it personally."

"Good to know," Axyl responded. "Don't bug Charlie and don't take her rudeness personally."

I scowled at both of them and they laughed like they'd been friends for years instead of this side of twenty-four hours.

"What's there to do around here?" Axyl asked when they finished laughing at my expense.

Brant held out an arm wide to encompass the lake and surrounding forest. "What you see is what you get. We have kayaks, fishing, there's a rope swing up that canyon, some cliffs, and some nice hikes. What are you into?"

I blocked out their get-to-know-you chatter, concentrating on my poetry until I heard Brant mention college.

I tried to pretend like I wasn't listening, but his words were knives in my chest and I couldn't breathe. I sucked in a lungful of air and swallowed. The result was the hiccups. My body bounced again and again with each one.

"You okay?" Axyl asked, peering at me, concern and amusement etched on his face.

"She's fine," Brant assured him. "She has anxiety and gets the hiccups when she feels an attack coming on."

What was he talking about?

"No, I...*hiccup*...don't," I growled.

"Whatever you say Charlie," Brant told me. His words said he was backing down, but he wasn't really. He was pacifying me.

I hate that.

Anger boiled inside me and had my heart racing for a different reason. This racing was more manageable. I looked at Brant. Really looked. He watched me with equal interest and a satisfied smile tugged at the corners of his mouth when he knew my hiccups were gone.

My anger turned to awe that he had played me so perfectly. How could he know me so well? No one knows me. And yet he had that anxious feeling evaporating into steam that dissipated with the afternoon sun like the dew on the tips of the long grasses surrounding the lake until the suffocating feeling was gone.

"So, Charlie," Axyl said, turning all his attention on me. "What's so great about the lake that it's your favorite place on Earth?"

I shrugged. Words suddenly failed me as his piercing gaze triggered something physiological in me and I felt wet under my arms. Sweat beaded up and rolled like a marble down the middle of my back. Was my face red too? I wanted to put a hand on my cheek to check for burning because the pleasant day was now scorching.

What was wrong with me? Maybe I was coming down with something.

I knew Brant was watching our exchange. If he knew me as well as he had proven he did just moments ago, he knew my temperature was on the rise. He'd get a kick out of that, attributing it to a crush on my parent's best friend's youngest son.

But that's not what it was. Axyl had laughed in my face. He wouldn't understand the beauty of the lake. I didn't have a crush on him! I didn't even like him.

"You have eyes and a brain, Axyl," I said. "At least I assume you do. You can figure it out on your own."

Brant and Axyl reared back in surprise. Brant's brows furrowed in confusion while Axyl laughed at me. Again.

"What's up with you today, Charlie?" Brant asked, coming to his feet and stepping toward me. "You're not yourself." He lunged at me then saying, "But I know how to change that."

My eyes went huge at his implication. I knew what was coming. In the blink of an eye- faster than I knew Brant could move- I was over his shoulder.

"No, Brant!" I resisted. "Put me down!" What would Axyl think when I surfaced as a drowned rat?

I beat on Brant's back with my free hand. If I didn't have the stupid notebook I could....*My notebook!* My fighting intensified. "Brant, my notebook! You'll ruin it!"

"I'll take that," Axyl said, snatching it from my hand.

"Nooo!" I screamed as Brant chucked me into the lake.

Bailey *would* pick that exact moment to prance onto the scene.

My head popped out of the water and I coughed once. Treading water, I pushed my hair out of my face. "Thanks a lot, Brant," I hollered. But there wasn't really anger behind it. The little dip in the lake was exactly what I needed to regulate my body temperature and get my head right again.

He grinned down at me with self-importance. "You're welcome. It's good to have you back."

"Axyl," Bailey purred, putting a possessive arm around his sculpted bicep. "Let's ditch these two." She watched me swim toward them. A disgusted look marred her pretty face. "I know a spot up that canyon you *have* to see."

I hefted myself onto the dock in time to snatch my notebook from Axyl as Bailey pulled him away. He looked like he might protest leaving, but he didn't say anything. That's the power of Bailey.

"Thanks for this," I said with a triumphant smile, waving my notebook in the air.

Good riddance. Maybe they'd all leave me in peace.

Brant chuckled. "I know what you're thinking."

"You're leaving, too?" I asked hopefully, turning on my brightest smile.

Brant chuckled again, but conceded. "I'll leave you alone."

I watched him walk up the dock to trail after Bailey and Axyl, all ease and self-confidence.

"Give him a chance, Charlie," he hollered as he went. "He's ok."

"How would you know?" I called to his retreating form. "You don't even know him."

"Neither do you." He turned and gave me a pointed look that said I should withhold judgment until I knew Axyl better.

But what was the point? He'd be leaving in thirteen days. I'd never see him again.

And he'd laughed at me.

Prey to My Body

My heart beats erratically like a hunted rabbit looking for an escape.

I swim toward the surface, never to reach it. And the pressure in my chest intensifies.

My breath comes in shallow gasps like a fish out of water-sides heaving.

I dip my toe in the clear edge of the lake and I can't fill my lungs.

37

Panic like I've never known clouds my mind until I need to run. But I can't run fast enough or far enough to escape the lion snapping at my shredded heels.

I arrive at the edge- calm on the surface, but roiling down deep. The water engulfs me and I give in to the undeniable screams and cries thrashing and clawing their way up my throat. They choke me.

The lake can't save me.
Irrational. Logically, I know this.
But I don't understand it. Like a nightmare, I can't stop it.
And I hate the power it has over me.

-The Skinny Tomboy

Chapter 5

The next day, I rested the kayak paddle across my lap and blinked in disbelief. *It couldn't be!*

When I opened my eyes, Axyl was still there. I watched with dread as he approached in his own borrowed kayak. Alone. His triceps contracted and his forearms bulged as he dipped his paddle into the lake on one side of the kayak and then the other, propelling him closer.

I frowned. *What was he doing out here? Where was Brant?*

"Whatcha doin' out here?" he called when he was one hundred feet from me.

"I could ask you the same thing," I called back, ignoring the way my heart rate traitorously kicked it up a notch. There was no doubt about it, he made me anxious. And not in a good way.

He paused mid-stroke with his paddle in the air. "What?" he yelled. I'd imagine most girls thought his face screwed up in confusion gave him a cute, innocent, boyish look, but not me.

I rolled my eyes and shook my head, letting him know I wasn't going to keep shouting back and forth. I glanced up at the sky so I wasn't caught staring at him. Soon, his kayak bumped mine softly and he put a hand on it to keep us together.

"Do you always spend so much time alone?" he asked, curiously.

"Do you always bug people?"

He flinched. "Ouch. Has anyone ever told you you're unapproachable?"

I paused, giving his question honest thought. I shook my head. I wasn't unapproachable. Bailey was all prickly and sarcastic. Bailey was unapproachable. I wasn't.

I heaved a sigh.

"In answer to your spending time alone question- yes. I like spending time out here without *distractions*. It helps me think."

He eyed me and gave a satisfied nod as if my answer confirmed his suspicions. "Unapproachable." When I made a noise of protest, he pointed at me. "That was two thinly veiled hints for me to jump in the lake in..." he looked at his Apple watch, "under a minute."

Grudgingly, I laughed because he'd caught my nonverbal, and apparently non-subtle, hints. "No. You asked. I told." Although I wouldn't mind if he jumped in the lake.

"Fair enough," he answered with another decided nod of his head. Then he tipped his dark head back and watched puffy clouds skim across the bright blue sky. "So, what do you think about?" he asked, studying the sky.

"What do I think about what?" I questioned, confused.

He looked at me briefly before his gaze returned heavenward. "You said being alone helps you think. So...what do you think about?"

"Oh. Life."

He scoffed and his eyes met mine again. "Care to narrow it down?"

What to say that wouldn't reveal too much, or worse, sound dumb? "I think about...names."

His face screwed up in confusion. "Names?"

Great. Dumb it is.

Well, I couldn't remain silent now. Ugh. I pulled the ball cap lower on my head and studied my paddle. "For example, when I have kids, I'm going to think seriously about what name I give them. It's a big deal, you know? Those people who name their kids Dusty when their last name is Rhodes or Rusty with the last name of Tubbs shouldn't be allowed to have kids.

A surprised laugh burst from Axyl. "No one would name their kids either of those names."

"Wanna bet?" I challenged, peering up at him from under my hat. "Look it up."

He was silent, digesting that.

"Or, you could be a skinny, tomboy *girl* and have the name Charlie," I muttered.

He studied me. "OK. Honestly? I was surprised when we pulled up and Charlie turned out to be a girl."

Yeah. He'd laughed in my face. And I suddenly remembered why I didn't like him. I plunged my paddle into the water and prepared to move to any other part of the lake where he wasn't.

But he kept his hand firmly on my kayak.

"I was dreading this trip," he confided, "thinking I'd have to be best buddies with the kids of some friends my parents knew twenty years ago. I was feeling the pressure."

I grunted. That didn't excuse his rude behavior.

"Aside from me turning out to be a girl, how is this situation any different from what you pictured?" I asked.

He lifted a shoulder. "I'm not sure. But it's different. I mean, your brother has been cool so far. Besides... I'm named after a car part," he empathized with a self-deprecating grin.

As far as I was concerned, his name was more *sexy* than automotive. Er...I mean...I would bet my humanitarian trip to Mexico next summer that girls thought his name sounded sexy. I didn't. But that didn't mean I couldn't understand his dislike of his name. Against my better judgment, I found myself commiserating. "The struggle is real."

He grinned over at me and my heart went crazy. "See? If you would quit fighting it, we are bound to be friends."

I lowered my eyes from his too-straight, mesmerizing smile and stared at the water. *Friends? I don't think so.* "Now let's not get crazy. Just because you and Brant already have a bromance going on, doesn't mean we are going to be friends."

I heard Axyl chuckle right before he swept his paddle across the top of the water, spraying me with cold lake. I sucked in a startled breath and stared at him. His heartstopping grin, this time mischievous, threw me yet again. But when he raised his brow smugly, clearly challenging me, I glared at him fiercely and growled as I slipped my paddle under his kayak and lifted.

His laughter echoed across the lake. "No way am I going to let a *skinny tomboy* swamp my kayak." And to prove he wasn't scared of me, he leaned back in his kayak with his hands clasped behind his head and sighed like he didn't have a care in the world.

His words stung worse than the cold water, but I only had paybacks on my mind. Using my kayak as leverage, I pushed at his kayak with my other hand, causing it to rock.

The only indication that the rocking concerned him was the slight surprise that filled his eyes. I pushed harder and he sat forward, his hand coming down swiftly to grab my paddle. A tug-of-war ensued.

"You're pretty strong," he grunted, pulling my paddle and my kayak along. "For an unapproachable girl."

I growled at him under my breath and pulled back on my paddle with all I had. When I felt him pull harder to counteract my surprising strength, I let up suddenly and watched as his body weight shifted in the opposite direction and his kayak tipped and capsized. His startled cry and flailing arms were too hilarious. My laughter came out in one loud burst.

Seconds later, his head broke through the surface, sending water spraying around us.

I held my paddle over my head with both hands, pumping it into the air. "Skinny girls rule!" I shouted through my laughter.

"Oh yeah?" he asked, righting his kayak and pulling himself on. And of course he looked great doing it. I would have looked like a malnourished whale trying to flop aboard a boat. "We'll see who's laughing when-"

"Hey, Ax," Bailey cooed, coming alongside us on her paddle board and interrupting whatever threat Axyl was about to make that I knew would be more enjoyable for me than he probably intended. We both stared as she gracefully lowered herself to her knees from a standing position down onto the board, letting her shiny hair cascade over her shoulders as she tilted her head back with closed eyes to bask in the sun.

Good grief! She was like a freaking ad for PacSun or something in that barely-there bikini with the sun reaching down for her like it depended on her for light and life instead of the other way around. Her glowing, golden skin rivaled the shimmering lake in impressiveness. Everything surrounding us was now a backdrop enhancing her natural beauty.

Life just wasn't fair.

And though Axyl's eyes never strayed lower than her shoulders, he clearly saw her. Who wouldn't? Especially when the alternative was sitting next to him in a faded suit and cutoffs and a weathered ball cap. Glamorous was not in my vocabulary. It wasn't even in my dictionary.

I plunged my paddle deep into the lake and turned for the dock.

"See you later, Axyl," I called over my shoulder.

"Uh, yeah. Whatever," came his reply.

Uh, huh. He was barely aware I'd left. I'd known it would happen.

Life *definitely* was not fair.

•••••

"Can we sit?"

I looked up from my dinner plate and swallowed a sigh with my bite of masticated food.

"You don't have to ask her all the time," Brant told Axyl, pushing my shoulder so I'd scoot and make room on the porch steps. "Just sit. She'll get over it."

Axyl stepped around us and took a seat a few steps below us, placing his plate on the stair just above him. "But she's so unapproachable," he replied with a grin and a wink up at me. To soften his words, I guessed. I was undecided on whether or not it was working. "I'm trying to make friends here, not enemies."

Brant howled with laughter. "With Charlie? Yeah. Good luck with that. *Unapproachable*?" He laughed again. "Perfect description of Charlie."

I glanced up from my plate at Brant. He thought so too? Was I really that cold and prickly? No. I wasn't.

"You should see her at school," Brant said. "We were at the same school the past two years and I don't think I saw her talking to anyone besides teachers and me the entire two years."

"That's not true," I argued as I picked at my salad. "You weren't with me every second. I talked to people." Though I couldn't think at the moment *who* exactly.

"Who?" Brant challenged like he'd read my mind.

"Yeah. Who?" Axyl chimed in. Brant grinned. He was enjoying having someone to help him fight his battles.

"You two are so obnoxious," I said, taking another bite of dinner.

They both laughed and fist bumped each other.

"What did you do after you hurried away from the lake this morning?" Axyl asked me after a time.

Brant looked between us. "Why would Charlie hurry away from the lake?"

Axyl grinned up at me. "She was afraid of retaliation."

I rolled my eyes and shoved another bite of food into my mouth. *Right. Like I was afraid of him.* I wasn't. But having Bailey for a sister had taught me to pick my battles. I could barely handle Bailey by herself. Being with both of them at the same time would be torture. And not only from beauty overload.

Brant kept eyeing us. "Retaliation?"

"Your tomboy little sister is pretty tough," Axyl replied with something like admiration in his voice.

I choked on my food and reached for my glass of homemade Root Beer. The fizz tickled my nose and made my eyes water. Perfect.

Brant chuckled and gave me a token pounding on the back. "She likes to think she is. Is that why you came back wet?" he asked Axyl. "I couldn't figure out how you'd fallen into the lake. Unless you're really that clumsy."

Axyl laughed and they were off sharing embarrassing stories of must-see-to-believe mishaps with each other.

I kept my eyes on my plate as I chewed on Brant's words. Axyl wet? If he had stayed out on the lake with Bailey, he would have been dry by the time they'd headed back. So he hadn't stayed out there with Bailey? Why? They were basically a carbon copy of each other. Of course they'd want to stick together. But he'd come back soon after I had? It didn't make sense.

I squashed down the seed of hope that not all of the male species were susceptible to Bailey's charms. But it was persistent and fought to find a spot of fertile ground in my chest.

Nope. Not going there.

Your Charlatan
It creeps in like an unwelcome, invading cancer.

Slowly. Silently. Catching you unaware.

Eating at your insides little by little until they aren't your own anymore.

Subtle.

Like pouring water into a vessel drop by drop, you realize it has filled you.

Wanting. Longing.

It's opaque but seems harmless until it overflows and there is no stopping it. No containing it.

Out of control. You are out of control.

But it seems familiar. Like family. You give a little more. It wears you down.

The flaxen cord tightens around your neck like a noose.

You are trapped. Aren't you?

Where will it leave you?

Cold and alone on the shore. Stripped bare. A shell of what you used to be.

But you've had a taste and part of you wants it, hopes for what it could become even though you know it will destroy you— heart and soul.

What if you do it?

Just go for it?

Its mocking voice invites you to take the plunge. And you do. Falling headlong into the scalding water below.

And you drown without even knowing you're gone.

And you'd only begun to live.

-The Skinny Tomboy

Chapter 6

"Hey, Smart Girl," someone called the next day.

I looked over my shoulder as Josh from a few cabins down strolled onto the dock.

I lifted a hand to shield my eyes from the sun. "Are you talking to me?" I asked.

He grinned, revealing a slightly crooked front tooth. "You're the smart one, aren't you?"

As opposed to whom? I didn't know what his definition of smart was or who he was comparing me to, so I just shrugged.

"Why do you always carry around that notebook?"

"What makes you think I always carry it around?" I asked.

His only response was a knowing grin. So, he'd been watching me? 'Cause that wasn't creepy. I fought against the urge to shudder.

"Is this your idea of a conversation?" I asked. One where you reveal stalker tendencies and do a lot of leering.

"What? Because I smiled?"

So he was stupid as well as creepy. Except that I was pretty sure he knew what he was doing. And that made him ten times more creepy!

"Maybe I'm trying to let you know I'd like to get to know you better?"

Yup. Definitely knew what he was doing. I gazed off across the lake, pretending he wasn't taking a seat next to me. Hopefully if I ignored him, he'd go away.

But like with the pesky deer flies, I couldn't be so lucky.

"Who's the girl you're always with?" he asked in the face of my silence.

Since my sister was the only other girl I'd ever had the misfortune to stand side by side in this spot, I knew he was probably talking about Bailey. And as much as I didn't understand her, I wasn't giving out any information to this weirdo about her, so I played dumb. "What girl?"

"The girl with the really hot bo...swimming suit."

My eyes narrowed. "You're not very subtle, are you?"

Again with the irritating grin.

I full-on glared at him now.

"And you're not very friendly, are you?" he countered with a slow smile. "But that's okay."

"If you mean because I'm not encouraging someone like you, then no."

Shock registered in his eyes for a split second before he flashed that seductive grin again. I despised that grin. Wanted to throw up on it. "Someone like me," he mumbled contemplatively before asking, "Is she your sister?"

I'm not a violent person. Ok. Let's not kid ourselves. I'm not even a confrontational person. But throat punching Josh suddenly sounded very appealing -what with all the questions and innuendo about my underage, albeit hot, sister. Yes. A swift throat punch would work. I mean aside from the puking all over him thing.

And he just had to keep talking. "You two don't look anything alike."

Yeah. I get that a lot, I thought wryly.

"What do you want, Josh?" I demanded. Ignoring him hadn't worked, so I went for direct. Unfortunately, it seemed to have the opposite effect of what I was going for.

"You remembered," he answered softly, looking pleased. "That's good," he assured me when I fired up my glare again. "Very good." He hopped up from the dock with more agility than I thought him capable of possessing. His body didn't exactly scream fit with the little roll around his waist. "I'll see you around."

As he walked away, I finally gave in to the shudder. I hadn't told him anything, yet somehow I worried I'd told him enough.

Great.

A few moments later, I felt the dock shift as someone else stepped onto it and headed my direction, if the sound of footsteps getting louder was any indication. I sighed in exasperation. Was it midday rush hour at the lake or something?

I kept my head lowered over my notebook. If I didn't engage, maybe whoever it was would go away.

"What's with the book?" Axyl asked, dropping down beside me on the dock.

And maybe not.

I sighed.

Man, he was everywhere! Why couldn't he just leave me alone? I looked up hoping to see Brant sitting next to Axyl, but Axyl was alone. Again. Where the heck was Brant anymore?

I lowered my eyes and fiddled with my pen as I debated about whether or not to ignore him. Maybe he'd get bored and go away. Then I remembered yesterday and sighed. Instead of acting uninterested in my simpleminded talk of names, he'd drawn me out and we'd ended up in a battle on the lake.

Then Bailey had shown up in all her glory.

I cringed as I recalled the scene and how Axyl hadn't remembered I existed after that.

My rebellious mind yelled at me that it was partly my fault because I'd given in too quickly the day before and fled. What good reason had there been for me to stay? Self-preservation, I argued, was not giving in.

Besides, according to Brant, Axyl had come back soon after I paddled away from him and Bailey when he easily could have spent the entire day with her. And Brant seemed to think he was an okay person.

I frowned. Brant could get along with anyone and, therefore, wasn't a reliable judge.

But in an effort to be more...approachable- as I'd been called the opposite by multiple people in the past few days, and since he didn't give me the creeper vibe like good old Josh- I would play nice.

I placed my pen in the book with yet another audible sigh and looked up. "What do you mean?"

He leaned closer, eyeing the pages of my notebook. I snapped the book shut.

"It's not a novel," he observed, sitting back. "But you carry it around like an extra appendage."

He'd noticed?

"Is it your diary?" He waggled his eyebrows at me.

Despite myself, I chuckled and shoved his shoulder. "You are as annoying as Brant. And no. It's not my *diary*." I emphasized the word as if I was scandalized at the thought.

Axyl laughed.

Maybe that's why I bobbed my head back and forth and admitted, "I dabble in poetry."

"You *dabble*," he repeated with a raised brow. "Define dabble."

I shrugged. "You know, participating in something in a casual way. *Dabble*. It's something I like to do when I have spare time." I tilted my head and raised a brow. "I'd think as someone interested in attending college, you'd at least be familiar with the word."

Axyl sat back on the dock, supporting himself with his hands. "There she is," he said with a satisfied smirk.

My brows pulled together and I looked around expecting to see Bailey, but there was no one.

I dragged in a breath when I realized he was looking at me. "What?" I had to ask.

"You," he replied with a teasing grin.

"What about me?" I asked warily.

"Aside from a couple well placed sighs, you allowed me to sit down and engage in conversation without forcing it out of you. For a minute there, I wondered where the real Charlie had gone."

My mouth opened and shut. "What...I don't..." I cleared my throat and capped and uncapped my pen. "I don't know what you're talking about."

Axyl nodded, his smirk filling out to become a real smile. "Right. You were saying..."

I shook my head. "Anywaaay. As I was saying. I like to write poetry. I'd never win any awards, but that's not why I do it."

"You won't win awards because you don't submit any of your stuff, or you won't win awards because it's not good enough to win if you were to submit it?" He smiled to show he was teasing.

I shoved him again and his smile widened. I hated that I kind of liked that smile when it wasn't laughing at me. Which wasn't often. So basically I didn't care for the smile. Not much.

"I'd never submit it," I told him. "It's...personal. You wouldn't understand."

"I won't pretend I know where someone would submit poetry for an award," he admitted. "But if it's good, you should let others be changed by it."

I laughed now. "You're funny. It is not 'changing lives' quality."

"How do you know?" He held out a hand. "Let me read some and I'll tell you if I'm a changed man."

I didn't have to look at him to picture his sculpted muscles. He may only be nineteen, but I would agree he was more man than boy.

My face burned at the thought and I hugged the book to me and shook my head.

"Oh, come on. I won't laugh. I promise."

Again, I shook my head because he had no problem laughing at me.

Thankfully, he let the subject drop and leaned back on his hands to survey the lake and the tall grass and trees that surrounded it on two sides. "You come here every summer?"

I nodded. "Yeah. It's my favorite place in the world."

Axyl reached a hand out and flicked a deer fly off my bare shoulder. He left goosebumps in its place, and I rubbed a hand up and down my arm to shoo them away.

"And you still haven't told me why." He swatted at another fly. "Even with the flies?" he asked wryly.

"By the second day, I hardly notice them anymore."

He looked at me, doubt filling his eyes. And I knew what he was thinking. He'd already been here four days.

Ten more days to go, I reassured myself. Then I'd never see Axyl Stewart again. Funny, I didn't feel as relieved by that as I thought I would. Despite the fact that he'd laughed at me and never left me alone, I found myself intrigued by him. I didn't want to. But he was surprisingly easy to talk to. And my *unapproachable*-ness hadn't kept him away. I didn't know how I felt about that.

"It must take me longer to acclimate," he replied. "I think my legs are one big, itchy bite," He ran a hand down his tan, toned calf. I quickly averted my eyes so I wouldn't be caught staring at the way the light brown hair shone in the sunshine. "And I'm not exaggerating when I tell you I still feel every stinking one." Then he gave me a sideways glance. "But this place could grow on you."

There was a tone in his voice I didn't understand.

"Where's your boyfriend?" I asked.

One side of Axyl's mouth went up. "You mean Brant?"

"Who else?"

Axyl jumped to his feet. I blew out a relieved breath. Oh, good. He was leaving.

"You're pretty funny, Charlie," he said, nudging my leg with the toe of his shoe. I swatted him away like the annoyance he was. "He said something about some friends on the other side of the lake."

I nodded, knowing Brant had probably gone to see the group he'd been cliff jumping with the other day.

When he didn't make a move to leave, but stared across the lake instead, I asked, "And you didn't go with him? I didn't think you two could stand to be apart."

His eyes focused down on me. "You really are funny," he repeated. Then he held up his hand. "I promise I won't tell anyone. If they knew, they'd never leave you alone."

"Kind of like how you never leave me alone?" I asked, squinting up at him. It was ridiculous how the sun glowed around him. I hoped he'd take the hint my words were intended to be and leave.

But his lips twitched and I got the distinct impression that I amused him. No one ever told me I was funny. He was obviously making fun of me again. I raised a hand to shield my eyes.

"It must be a pain to actually have to interact with people," he commented.

He had no idea.

He toed off his shoes and I frowned in consternation. Now what was he doing? I could have sworn he was going to leave me alone. Was it too much to ask for him to please leave me alone?

When he reached down to tug off his shirt, my eyes cut to the lake. Not only did I not need the mental image of a shirtless Axyl, I didn't want it.

His phone landed with a thunk on the dock beside me, right next to his abandoned shirt. I glanced up in time to see him cannonball into the water.

"Are you going to make me swim alone?" he asked after he'd surfaced and shaken the excess water from his hair.

"I'm not making you do anything," I replied. "You jumped in all on your own."

"It's not safe to swim alone."

"Then you shouldn't have jumped in." I opened my notebook and shoved the end of the pen in my mouth.

"What if I get a cramp? Would you save me?"

I closed my eyes. "I was wrong before. You're not as annoying as Brant. You're *more* annoying than Brant." Much more.

"So you're saying you'd let me drown?" he asked. His voice sounded closer- and more pathetic- than before.

I opened my eyes to see him resting his folded arms on the dock, peering up at me with sad eyes.

Oh, brother.

My lips twitched, but I clamped down on them, refusing to give into a smile like I would with my brother.

I tucked my pen in my notebook. "You are so ridiculous," I finally said, inserting as much distaste into my voice as I could muster.

Now his lips twitched and I hated that I watched, hoping they would widen into a full smile.

Bailey, I chanted. *He's Bailey.* I grabbed my notebook and hopped to my feet, intending to leave him to his fate in the water and find a more quiet spot to compose. Away from smiling lips and eyes that saw too much.

"Yes! I knew you couldn't resist," he crowed.

"That's where you're wrong," I said, turning to leave. "I'm not swimming. I'm...." my voice trailed off and I paused midstep when I saw that guy Josh standing on his cabin porch watching me.

"You're what?"

I faintly heard Axyl questioning me, but I didn't respond. I was too busy trying to decide if it would be better to hurry to our cabin, knowing Josh could follow and chat me up again- he seriously gave me the creeps- or if I should jump into the lake with Axyl.

Decided, I unbuttoned my shorts and let them drop to the dock before sliding my feet from my flip flops. My breath caught in my lungs as I dove head first into the cool water.

I quickly surfaced and swam toward a grinning Axyl.

"You won with the kayaks yesterday," he said, "but we'll see who wins the battle of strength today."

His wicked grin only made me hesitate for a moment. I glanced over my shoulder to see Josh now standing on their front lawn. Closer than before. I pushed through the water toward Axyl with determined strokes.

I'd take the lesser of two evils even if that meant having to interact with Bailey's twin in male form. At least he was only annoying. I couldn't say as much for Josh.

•••••

"You ready, Bailey?" Brant asked as he stood from the table and took his plate to the sink.

Mom looked up from the puzzle she and Kristin were putting together and asked, "Where are you two headed?"

If there was surprise in her voice at Brant willingly spending time with Bailey, I was the only one who heard it.

"Let me grab my purse," Bailey told Brant, swallowing the last bite of her lunch as she headed for the loft. "We are walking into town," she said to Mom over her shoulder.

But her smile was too pleased. And *walking* into town? Bailey? What was she up to?

"I wanted to see if they got any more of those little summer dresses in stock," Bailey reported.

I peered at Bailey through narrowed eyes. Yeah. Bailey liked clothes, but her smile wasn't over a dress. And she'd sooner jump in the lake than walk when Brant could take her in the car. What was it?

My answer walked into the living room just then. Like me, he'd changed out of his swimming suit, but his hair was still wet.

"Are you going too?" Kristin asked Axyl, looking pleased. But what mom wouldn't be happy that her best friend's kids and her son were getting along?

"Yeah," he replied, scanning the room until he found me. "You're coming, too, right Charlie?"

I paused mid chew of my sandwich and stared around the room like a deer stuck in the headlights. I'd had enough peopling today, what with talking with Josh and then swimming with Axyl. But I had to hand it to him, he was an amazing swimmer. He easily beat me in two of the three races we swam and he didn't even tease me about it. Well, not too badly. But that still didn't mean I like him.

Bailey grabbed Axyl's arm. "Charlie doesn't like shopping."

Brant snorted. "Can you blame her? The only reason I'm going with you two is to price those knee boards."

"You should see if they do rentals," I suggested.

Brant nodded, considering my comment and then said, "Some of the guys on the other side of the lake have a boat. They said we could go out later today."

"Awesome!" Axyl exclaimed. "A boat? I'm there." He and Brant bumped fists and I smirked. The bromance was alive and well. Boys were so dumb.

"You should come, Charlie," Brant said.

I swallowed. "Into town or on the boat?" I asked. Neither sounded very appealing.

"To town," Brant said at the same time Axyl said, "Both."

Brant looked at Axyl and shrugged. "Well, yeah. Both I guess. You like kayaks. Why not boats? I'll have to check with the guys though. I don't know how much room they have."

"And ask if there's room for me," Bailey pouted, hanging on Axyl's arm.

Brant watched her and frowned. "I'll see." But he didn't sound hopeful that there would be room for all of us.

"That's okay. Bailey can go," I offered. "Thanks for the invite though." Brant frowned as Bailey beamed.

"Well, what are we waiting for?" Bailey asked, dragging Axyl across the room. "Let's go."

Brant looked at me, silently questioning one last time whether or not I wanted to go with them into town. Or was it pleading? I looked at Bailey and Axyl and back at Brant with an exaggerated eye roll and shook my head. He frowned at me. He didn't want to go either, I knew. But by the determined look on his face, he didn't trust Bailey or he didn't trust Axyl, one or the other. And he wasn't letting them go anywhere alone together.

"Have fun," Mom hollered after Brant.

"Yeah," I giggled. "Have fun."

Brant shot me a death glare and shoved through the door.

"Hey, Brant?" I called him back, barely containing my laughter.

He poked his head back into the cabin. "Yeah?"

"Don't let the door slam."

Chapter 7

Brant's new friends had given the okay for all of us to join them on the boat. So the four of us grabbed our towels and sunscreen after dinner and wandered to the other side of the lake where the boats were docked. The sun was still high enough in the sky that we'd get a few hours of boating in before we had to call it a day.

The dusty road clung to my sandaled feet and ankles as we walked. I slung my towel over my shoulder and wished for my notebook to capture the contrast between the oppressive, dry heat of the trail and the cool spray of the water that I knew awaited me past the dock. I couldn't wait to feel the wind whipping through my hair.

We followed Brant since he seemed to know where we were supposed to meet the group. We clomped down the dock and stopped in front of a sleek white boat with the words *Siren of the Sea* painted across the side in glittering seafoam green lettering.

A brown-haired guy who looked to be about Brant and Axyl's age in swim shorts and deck shoes hopped lithely off the boat to the dock and touched his knuckles to Brant's.

"You made it," the guy said with an easy smile, looking us over.

"Charlie, Axyl, and Bailey, this is Coleman," Brant said. "Thanks for letting us come."

"No problem," Coleman replied with that easy smile. "Everyone else is here, so let's get going."

No one had to tell Brant twice. He vaulted himself onto the boat and greeted the others waiting there. Bailey and I weren't as sure-footed. Coleman held out a hand to assist Bailey and then me. The boat rocked gently back and forth with the added weight and I shifted from side to side on unsteady land legs and sat down hard on the bench seat near two Bailey-type girls. One was a tall blonde and the other had long, darker hair. Both were suitable for boat ads. Apparently, the world was full of beautiful people. And they were all here at the lake this summer. I didn't like them instantly, figuring them both to become best friends with Bailey before the day was over.

Brant introduced us to Parker, Duncan, Laney, and Iris while Coleman and Axyl took care of the ropes and shoved us off. I knew I wouldn't remember their names, and I knew they probably didn't care about mine, but I smiled a hello anyway.

Coleman stood at the wheel and we slowly trolled out of shallow water. It wasn't long before we were skimming at high speeds across the lake in the power boat. The wind and spray of the water were as refreshing as I'd imagined they'd be. My fingers itched for my notebook and pen.

"How often do you come to the lake?" the blonde- Iris, I thought- asked.

"Every summer," I replied over the wind. "We have a cabin on the other side of the lake."

She nodded her understanding.

I knew I should follow up her question with one of my own, but I'd never been good at small talk. I couldn't get my mind and mouth to match up. My mind was a blank sheet of paper. I thought she'd give up, but she turned to me again a few minutes later.

"Axyl's really good," she observed with a nod out to the water. "Are you sure he's never done knee boarding before?"

I shrugged. "That's what he said."

"He's fun to watch."

I glanced at Iris, trying to decipher her meaning. Her face showed open interest. I couldn't blame her. She only saw what the rest of the world saw when they gazed upon Axyl Stewart.

We both watched him lean left, then right, causing the knee board to slide across the surface of the lake on one side of the boat and then the other. He looked like a pro out there. It wouldn't be long before he was attempting flips. He gave us a thumbs up which we relayed to Coleman so he could pick up the speed a bit.

When Duncan was ready to go out, Coleman whipped the boat dangerously to the right and created a counter wave that sent Axyl sideways. He let go of the rope and sank into the lake. The guys cheered like the wipeout had been part of the ride and Coleman hadn't purposely sunk Axyl.

When everyone who wanted a turn on the knee board had taken one, Coleman steered the boat to a quiet cove, dropped the anchor, and killed the engine. The guys bailed over the sides of the boat and into the water. They laughed and splashed around. I had to admit, I was having a good time observing Brant's new friends. They didn't take people too seriously. If you were willing to have fun, they were willing to have you along.

Bailey and Laney cannonballed into the middle of the guys and more splashing ensued. Though it was now accompanied by girly squeals.

"You want something to drink?" Iris asked, moving to the front of the boat and grabbing a Coke from the cooler.

"A water?" I said.

She grabbed a bottled water and handed it to me.

"Thanks." I twisted the cap off and took a sip of cold water, swallowing it along with a healthy dose of nerves and asked, "How often do you come out on the lake?" I raised the bottle to my lips and took another sip.

"Coleman's family owns the cabin, so we come up a couple weekends every summer. They always bring the boat. We've been friends forever. It's nice." She closed her eyes and tilted her face toward the waning sun. "Brant's your brother, right?" I had a difficult time deciding if her tone was more hopeful or curious.

"Yeah," I replied.

She opened her eyes and looked at me, color rising in her face that I didn't think had anything to do with being in the sun.

"Is he seeing anyone?"

A smile tugged at the corners of my lips, but I didn't want to embarrass her more by laughing. "No. Who'd want to date my dumb brother?" I didn't think he was dumb, but he was...*Brant*.

She squirmed in her seat a little. "He's so hot," she whispered, glancing over her shoulder to make sure she wouldn't be overheard. But there was so much screaming and splashing in the water that she was safe.

Now I did laugh. "I guess. I mean other girls think he is."

"You're from Utah, right?"

"Yeah."

"Hmm. That's a ways from Colorado."

"Not too far," I pointed out. "We're neighbors."

"He's headed for college at the end of the summer?"

I gave her a sad smile. "Yeah."

"Oh well," she sighed wistfully.

I knew how she felt. I didn't want him to leave either. But then, *I'd* see him again eventually. I gave her another sad smile.

"How well do you know Axyl?" Iris asked, taking a sip of her Coke.

"Just met him," I admitted. "His mom and my mom were friends in high school. They are vacationing with us for a few days."

"He's cute too," she said.

"And he knows it," I muttered. But a little bit of doubt had wiggled its way into my brain since this afternoon, making me question if I truly believed my own words. Yeah, he had been overbearing during the impromptu swim races earlier, but his bravado was more teasing than real ego. If I was honest, he wasn't any worse than Brant would have been. And he had invited me to go into town with them after lunch. He had insisted I tag along with them tonight on the boat. He was putting a lot of effort into making me accept him considering how I repeatedly pushed him away.

"You don't like him?" Iris asked, sounding surprised.

I quieted the frown of deep thought that was on my face and shrugged. "He's like an annoying brother, but worse." I wasn't willing to give him the green light on friendship just yet, but after today he didn't seem as bad as Bailey. No one was as bad as Bailey though.

"But he's cute-annoying," Iris insisted.

"Hmmm." That was as committed an answer as I felt comfortable giving.

"That's Duncan for me," Iris admitted. "And we're too good of friends for me to think he's cute, so I understand what you're saying."

The gentle rocking of the boat and Iris' open, friendly personality worked their magic. I found myself relaxing into the seat and tucked my legs up under me. This was a new experience for me in more ways than one. And I didn't *not* like it.

"We're all going our separate ways for school in the fall," Iris continued, "so we put up with each other more than we normally would. You never know when the last time is really the last time you'll all be together, ya know?"

I nodded even though I didn't know as far as a group of friends went. But I did know how I felt about Brant leaving us. I hated it.

"Hey, Charlie," Brant shouted from the water, interrupting my and Iris' conversation. "What are you waiting for?"

I waved him off and rolled my eyes at Iris in a 'see what I mean' way. Annoying.

Iris grinned and took another swallow of her Coke.

"Well, I don't know about you," she said, setting the can on the floor and standing, "but I'm going to see if I can give your brother an excuse to visit Colorado." She grinned at me again and I found myself returning it.

Huh, I thought as I stood to follow Iris to the side of the boat. Maybe I wasn't completely broken after all.

"I'm coming in," Iris hollered as she launched herself over the side of the boat and into the water. Curious, I paid attention to her. While she interacted with the other guys, her eyes were definitely on Brant more than the others. She stuck closer to him and tried to engage him in conversation. I could easily see her partiality toward him. Her actions were similar to Bailey's, but more subtle, less desperate. She made it look so easy. It was like a gift that certain people are born with while others aren't. I very much wasn't.

I knew I couldn't be as smooth as Iris, but I also didn't want to be the only lame one still on the boat. Without thinking too much about it, I leaped overboard and swam toward Iris and Brant.

"'Bout time you joined us, Charlie Bucket," Brant teased. I looked at him in surprise. He hadn't called me that in years.

When Brant was ten and I was eight, we had a moderate obsession with the book *Charlie and the Chocolate Factory*. Mom read it to us every night before bed for weeks. When she finished, we begged her to read it again. I think we identified with it for some strange reason. Brant had a paper route, I loved chocolate and dreamed of winning a tour of a chocolate factory, and Bailey- even at a young age- reminded us of a mix of Veruca Salt and Violet Beauregarde. Maybe we shouldn't have encouraged her so much.

For months after school and on weekends, we'd pretend we were the characters and act out the story. Because there were only three of us, we had to take on many roles. Brant got to be Grandpa Joe and Willy Wonka because he was the oldest and a little strange besides. Because Bailey was a perfect fit for the roles of Violet and Veruca, that left me, among other characters, being Charlie.

Those were fun times. I had fond memories of those days. That's why I didn't mind that Brant called me Charlie Bucket. While Bailey called me Charles to tick me off, Brant's nickname for me, though rarely used, was said with love.

"You couldn't wait for me to do this..." He lunged at me and shoved me under water.

When I surfaced, I went after him. He laughed and skirted behind Iris, holding her at the waist in front of him like a shield.

"Leave it to my brother to hide behind a girl," I goaded.

Brant wiggled his eyebrows and grinned and I knew he wasn't embarrassed even a little bit about being close to Iris.

"If I wasn't behind her, I couldn't do this." His final words came out in a grunt as he picked Iris up by the waist and hefted her into the air. I turned to watch her squealing form flail and plunge into the water. Brant used the distraction to come at me and dunk me again.

"Do you need someone to save you?" Duncan asked when I surfaced. I frowned and watched as he positioned himself between me and my brother and made a show of shoving Brant away and then blocking him out with his arms spread wide.

"I can handle Brant," I told Duncan. "He's light work."

Brant snorted at my words and gave Duncan the slip, coming at me with determined strokes.

I turned, ready to put as much distance between us as possible, but grunted when I plowed into a hard chest. Strong hands wrapped around my waist, steadying me against his warm body and stealing my breath. I looked up into Axyl's startled face and blinked.

"Hold her there, Axyl," Brant called. "Here comes her light work."

"Take care of him for me," I said, pushing against Axyl. He released me like he'd been shocked. Cold immediately replaced the warmth where his hands had been, and I darted around him.

"Was it as terrible as you thought it would be?" Brant asked, slinging an arm across my shoulders as we made our way back around the lake on foot in the dark.

I felt my mouth turn up into a real smile as I thought about talking with Iris and messing around in the water with everyone.

"It was fun," I admitted, pulling my towel tighter around my body and in an effort to control my shivering. A jacket would have been nice right about now. The temperature had dropped with the sun and my suit wasn't completely dry yet. "And I don't have to ask you if you had a good time." I looked at him out of the corner of my eye and pulled my lips in to keep a smile at bay.

Brant stared straight ahead. "I don't know what you're talking about," he replied evenly. But the corners of his mouth twitched.

"I like her, Brant," I confided. "She's really nice."

"Not bad for a summer fling," he said.

I studied him for a moment, trying to discover his true feelings. When his eyes gave nothing away, I watched my feet take another step and then another on the dark road. "I've never understood that mentality," I finally responded with a shake of my head.

"What mentality?" he asked.

"It's like you're using someone for a few months to get what you can out of them and then you never think of them again. It seems heartless. I don't know how people do it."

"It's just about having a good time in the present. Living life to the fullest while you're in that moment." He made it sound so simple and uncomplicated.

"But how do you keep your heart from getting involved?"

"You're thinking too much. You make it all clear upfront. Then there are no hard feelings."

I shook my head again. "I couldn't do it. I know I'd read into it and wonder what it was about me that kept the guy from wanting something more permanent. I want to be unforgettable."

Brant reached up with one hand and squeezed my cheeks together so I had fish lips. "With this face, you're definitely unforgettable."

I shoved him away with a laugh.

"You only feel that way, Charlie, because you don't have any friends," Bailey said, inserting herself into the conversation from behind them. "If you had friends, you wouldn't cling so tight to whatever you can get."

Ugh. I had forgotten they were back there. "Thank you, Bailey," I muttered.

"You don't like people," Brant pointed out to me. "Why are you worried about it?"

"We're leaving for college anyway," Axyl quipped. "It would suck to be tied down."

"See?" Brant said, clearly feeling his way of thinking was right because he had Axyl backing him up.

Was it just guys who felt that way, or did women like surface relationships too? Just because I didn't put a lot of effort into meeting people didn't mean that I didn't want to. And when I finally found someone worth getting to know, I wanted to be certain he was as committed to being in a relationship as I was. I don't have extra reserves of emotion to waste them on a fling.

"Then you two better not spend any more time together," I said. "You seem pretty attached."

"Attached, huh?" Brant asked, suddenly throwing me over his shoulder. "Not as attached as I'm going to be to you." He spun in the gravel and I shrieked. "I'm going to stick so close to you that you'll beg me to leave you alone."

"I already do," I hollered, pounding on his back.

"You think it's been bad before?" Brant laughed. "It's going to be ten times worse. I might even move up into the loft."

Now I laughed. "No you wouldn't. Put me down!"

"Nope," Brant said, tightening his hold on my legs. "You have to play me in a round of SkipBo before you can go to bed."

"Fine. I want to make it clear upfront that I will win. No hard feelings, though, Brant."

"You in, Axyl?" Brant asked.

"I am," Bailey said, wrapping a hand around Axyl's bicep.

"You're all going down," I yelled from my very undignified position. "The blood is rushing to my head, Brant."

No response.

"I'm serious, Brant...I might get sick...Brant?...Brant!"

Chapter 8

"That place in town that I rented the boards from yesterday?" Brant said over breakfast the next morning. "They also rent bikes."

"Did someone open a new shop?" Mom asked.

Brant nodded. "Some out-of-towner saw a potential business venture and moved here. He rents anything from those inflatable water slides to bikes. Says he's crazy busy."

"That's good," Dad said.

"Why don't we ever think of things like that?" Mom asked Dad.

"I was thinking," Brant said, looking from me to Axyl, "that we should rent some bikes today and ride around the lake."

Axyl nodded. "Let's do it."

"You in, Charlie?" Brant asked.

I shrugged. "Why not."

"See if Bailey wants to go, will you?" Mom asked.

"She's still in bed," Brant said, rising from the table. "I wanted to leave now."

When Mom nodded, Axyl and I got up from the table and followed Brant to the sink with our dishes.

"Let me grab my phone," I told them. "I'll be back in a minute."

Three minutes later, I followed Brant and Axyl out the cabin door. We walked side-by-side down the dirt road in companionable silence. The morning wasn't hot yet, but it also wasn't cold. I raised my face to the sun, appreciating the warmth.

"What do you do at home for fun?" Brant asked Axyl after a few minutes.

Axyl shrugged. "Same thing everyone else our age does. Gaming, work, school, hanging out with friends."

Brant nodded. "Yeah. Me too." Then he shot Axyl a mischievous grin. "Ever helped haul away furniture…"

Axyl's brow rose. "What does that mean?"

"I don't know if people do this in Texas, but when people have furniture they don't want anymore here, sometimes they put it on the curb outside their house with a 'Free' sign on it instead of hauling it away to the dump." Axyl nodded his understanding. "If we see it while a group of us are out wandering around, we pick it up and move it to its new home."

"That's you?" I gasped. "I wondered why those chairs were in a circle around the light pole in the grocery store parking lot."

Brant laughed. "And the one at the bus stop. Yeah. There was a stack of them in front of a house over by the park. They looked sad outside all alone."

"I heard Mrs. O'Neal thank Mom for the new chair for her front porch the other day," I laughed. "Mom had no idea what she was talking about. Mrs. O'Neal is out there everyday now keeping track of the neighborhood."

"See?" Brant said. "Serving the community wherever I go."

"We've done that with Christmas trees, but not abandoned furniture," Axyl said.

"Christmas trees are fun," Brant agreed with a chuckle.

Before I knew it, we were standing in front of the rental shop. It looked more like a surf shack someone threw up in a hurry. But it fit in with the touristy atmosphere.

A guy about Brant's age looked up from the display of sun glasses he was restocking when the bell rang over the door.

"Back again," he said to Brant. "Hey, man." He nodded to Axyl before offering me an inviting smile. "Where are you picking up all the chicks?" he asked my brother, though his gaze lingered on mine. "Yesterday you had a blonde with you."

"My sisters," Brant informed him, frowning.

The guy held up both hands, his smile lowering a notch. "That's cool. How can I help you today?"

"We're here to rent some bikes."

After Brant signed and paid for the rentals, we walked outside to choose our bikes. Multiple colors of beach cruisers lined the sidewalk in a shiny row. I chose a light green one that reminded me of the lake and put on my helmet, adjusting the straps to fit.

"Which way?" Axyl asked, adjusting his helmet and putting on his sunglasses.

"Follow me," Brant said, pushing off the ground and starting down the street. Axyl and I fell into line behind him.

The comfortable morning breeze cooled a few degrees on the wind as we rode along. I felt light and free. "This was a good idea," I told Brant with a smile. "Why haven't we done it before?"

"I know," he replied. "You're welcome."

"This is going to take all day if we keep your pace,"Axyl said, moving alongside Brant.

"It's Charlie," Brant told him. "She's holding us back."

"Whatever," I grumbled. "You're welcome to go ahead."

Axyl pulled in front, swerving back and forth to keep Brant behind.

"Hey, Charlie," Brant hollered over his shoulder, "Your shoelace is untied."

Even though Brant had gotten me a million times with that lame joke, I still embarrassed myself by looking down to check my shoes. I scoffed when I saw I was wearing sandals. No laces. Ugh. Broth-

My thought was cut off with Brant's warning cry of, "Watch out, Charlie!" The rest of whatever he was going to say was drowned out by an insistent horn.

My eyes snapped up at all the noise and then widened in alarm. With a cry, I swerved off the road to avoid a collision with the runaway golf cart barreling toward me- the driver wildly waving his arms- and found myself careening out of control down the steep embankment leading to the lake. My eyes widened yet again as the front bike tire hit a rock and launched me over the handlebars and into the lake.

"Still think this was a good idea?" Brant asked, dragging himself and my bike up the embankment. A stream of water gushed from his soggy shoes and rolled back down the hill for home.

I followed him at a slower pace, mentally reviewing the last thirty seconds in my frazzled mind. Other than a wet phone, a mouth full of lake water and a few scratches, I was fine.

I rested my bike against my hip and squeezed the bottom of my t-shirt. Water ran from it in big drops to the road, darkening the dirt. "Sure. I needed an adventure today."

"Happy to help," Brant said, grinning and shaking his head like a dog to dry his hair.

"Is the bike okay?" I asked, leaning down to brush grass and leaves off my scraped shin.

Brant's eyes ran over our rentals as he picked his bike up off the ground where he had hastily tossed it aside when he jumped in the water after me. "They look fine. A scratch or two. Nothing major."

I nodded, taking the elastic out of my hair and brushing through it with my fingers before securing it on top of my head again in a messy bun.

"You two okay?" Axyl asked, skidding to a stop beside us and looking us over closely. "One minute you were there, and the next you were gone. What happened?"

"Charlie decided she needed to cool off after a game of chicken with a golf cart," Brant told him.

"There are easier ways," Axyl assured me.

Brant shook his head. "I tried to tell her…"

"You want to head back to the cabin?" Axyl asked, eyeing the road rash on my leg.

I looked to Brant. He shrugged, so I shook my head. "I'll dry off faster with wind," I said, slinging my leg over the bar and lifting onto the seat.

"Okay," Axyl said, straddling his bike. "Let's go."

"Try to stay on the road this time, huh, Charlie?" Brant called.

"If you'll lay off the stupid jokes, we'll be fine."

"How is this my fault?" he asked. "I saved your life. You should be thanking me. How about you do my chores until I leave for school?"

"Nice try," I said with a laugh.

•••••

A few hours later, clean and dry, Brant, Ayxl, Bailey and I stepped onto Coleman's boat.

"Everyone ask Charlie about her kamikaze into the lake this morning," Brant said with a grin.

We weren't even away from the dock yet and he was already humiliating me. My mouth dropped open and I shook my head. "They don't need to hear about that," I managed, glaring at Brant.

"But it makes me look so good," he said. "Tell them how I jumped in the water and saved you."

Axyl snorted a laugh. "Because she was in so much danger in water up to her knees."

"You can drown in an inch of water," Brant argued.

"I'll tell them how you saved me, Brant," I said. "Right after I tell them how your stupid joke distracted me in the first place."

Everyone but Bailey and Laney laughed. "She always has to be the center of attention," Bailey muttered to Laney.

I ignored her and went to take a seat by Iris.

"What really happened?" Iris asked.

"I opted for the lake instead of a head on collision with a golf cart," I told her.

"No way," she breathed.

I nodded. "I know it sounds made up, but..." I lifted my leg and pointed my toe to show her my shin.

"And she even managed a perfect swan dive," Brant said, joining us. "I would have given her a ten for sure. You know, if I hadn't been so worried about saving her life."

I rolled my eyes and Iris laughed.

"I'm glad you're okay," Duncan said, sitting beside me and draping an arm around my shoulders.

I offered him a polite smile, wishing I could get out from under his arm. We were crammed on the boat like sardines and I didn't have anywhere else to go.

I folded my arms to make myself smaller and listened to Brant and Axyl recount the harrowing events of the day. Brant was a great storyteller and had everyone's undivided attention. I found myself laughing along with the group as Axyl told about looking around and finding himself alone on the road when Brant and I had been right behind him seconds before.

Before I knew it, Coleman was steering the boat to the calmer spot we stopped at the other night and cutting the engine. Shirts came off and everyone bailed into the water except Iris and me.

"How's the annoying brother-type?" Iris asked, leaning in to not be overheard.

I glanced over the water until my eyes landed on Axyl. He was attempting to wrestle a football away from Brant. They were both laughing and trying to dunk each other. I hated that I noticed the way water droplets sparkled in the sun as it rolled down Axyl's bronze chest.

"By that sigh, I'd say he's not as annoying as he was a few days ago," Iris teased.

Great. I wasn't aware that my wistful sigh had been audible. I blushed and dragged my eyes away from Axyl, pretending fascination with the scenery.

"I sighed?" I asked, hoping the mortification I felt at being so transparent wasn't too apparent. "It wasn't really a sigh, it was..." I paused, searching for the right word, but came up empty.

Iris giggled. "That's what I thought."

"What did you think?" I asked, messing with the string on my jacket to avoid looking at her.

"You like him," she said in a sing-song voice.

I glanced at her before returning my gaze to my hands twisting the string around my finger in my lap. "Is it that obvious?" I asked quietly. Oh, how I hoped her answer was a big, fat no. "I have tried so hard not to, but I'm finding I can't help it." Why was he so...so...likable?

"It's not that obvious," she assured me. "I remembered what you said about him the last time we talked and you seem different tonight, so I wondered if something had changed."

I thought about her observation as she got up and grabbed a couple drinks out of the cooler. I was surprised when I realized I hadn't gotten angry at Axyl or Brant's teasing. But then, Brant had a way of spinning a story so it wasn't glaringly obvious that I was the pitiful lead role everyone should be laughing at. Although he didn't always, most of the time he had my back.

Iris handed me a soda and asked, "Why don't you want to like him?"

I shrugged. "It's like you and Brant. You live in different states, going away to school in a few months…" my voice trailed off. *Not to mention he'd never like someone like me.*

"I don't blame you. Too bad Bailey doesn't have the same reservations."

We both turned in time to see Bailey wrap an arm around Axyl's neck from behind and cling to his back. Brant wrestled the football from Axyl.

My heart stuttered to a stop. "You think he likes her?" I breathed.

"I can't tell how he feels, but she has definitely claimed him."

We watched Axyl wrap a hand around Bailey's wrist and remove her arm from his neck. Bailey used her free hand to shove Axyl's head under the water. He came up laughing and wiped his eyes. Bailey grinned and took his hand, holding it longer than was necessary. Laney tugged on his other arm to get his attention. I rolled my eyes. Poor Axyl. It was like piranha fighting over a chunk of meat.

Axyl pulled free from both of them and glanced over at the boat, doing a double take when he saw us watching him. He raised a brow, asking a silent question, then waved for us to get into the water. His eyes pled with us to help him.

"You should go," Iris said. "If he was asking me, you can bet I would be out there keeping Bailey and Laney away from him."

"What makes you think he was waving to me? It could have been you. Or both of us." I watched Brant shout 'heads up' and throw the football in the middle of Axyl, Bailey, and Laney. The girls shrieked and scattered, freeing Axyl.

Iris shook her head and grinned at me. "No. It's you," she said with confidence. "Besides, I might go flirt with Brant. Get it in while I can. Come on." I watched as she tugged off her shirt and slipped out of her shorts then dove off the side of the boat. She surfaced and swam to where Brant and the other guys were messing around.

Suddenly, the football sailed through the air and landed in the boat at my feet. I jumped, startled, but bent down and picked it up, looking over the water to see who threw it. Axyl shrugged and held his hands up in a gesture of innocence, but his grin gave him away. I frowned. He held his hands above his head and nodded, telling me to pass him the ball.

"Or can you not throw?" he teased.

My frown deepened and I wrapped my hand around the football, cocked my arm back and released the ball with as much force as I had.

I hoped it hit him in the head.

I laughed at his rounded eyes and need for quick reflexes as he caught the ball centimeters from his face.

When he moved the ball, he was grinning. His eyes met mine and he beckoned me to get in and join him with a flick of his head.

I shrugged and set my can down. It would be stupid to be the only one on the boat. I left my clothes on the seat and jumped in.

"Careful, Charlie," Brant teased as I swam closer. "You've already had one close call today."

"Thanks for your concern, Brant, but you should worry about yourself," I said, launching a wave of water at his face with my hand.

With a war cry that called in the troops, Brant returned fire. He sent a repeated barrage of water my way until the other guys had circled and I was getting it from all sides. I was surrounded.

I couldn't see, let alone breathe. Brant was right. I was going to drown if whoever was spraying me in the face kept at it. I was a bit disoriented, but I thought I remembered Brant's evil grin on the other side of the worst of the attack, so I surged forward blindly, wrapping my arms around his head, attempting to force him under. Our wrestling took me around behind him. I hopped on his back to get more leverage and pushed his head under again. Thankfully, by that time, the girls had joined the game, eliminating my other attackers.

"Beg for mercy, Brant," I said, opening my eyes. But it wasn't Brant who surfaced and turned his head to look at me over his shoulder with a villainous smile. My eyes widened in horror and I gasped, withdrawing my arms and legs from around him so quickly I went under. Axyl held me down for a few seconds with a hand on my head before grasping my bicep and raising me up until my head was above water.

I pushed backward, hands raised. "I didn't know it was you," I said.

Axyl chuckled, advancing. "Sure you didn't. First you try to take my head off with the football, then you try to drown me."

"The football? Yes." I nodded as he reached out for my wrist. I shoved his hand away and backed up again. "But the drowning…you have to believe me. I never would have gotten that close if I'd known it was you." And that was the absolute, honest truth. Because now that I knew it was him, I couldn't get the feel of being wrapped around him out of my mind. It wasn't a memory that needed repeating at will. I blushed just thinking about it.

He managed to grab my fingers and drag me to him even though I fought against it.

"Looks like you could use some help," Brant said, coming to my rescue.

I only had enough time to sigh in relief before Brant turned on me and I realized he'd been offering his help to Axyl, not to me. Taking advantage of Axyl as a distraction, he launched himself at me. With hands on both of my shoulders, he submerged us both.

"Don't help him," I shouted at Brant as soon as I surfaced. Axyl high-fived Brant, congratulating him like distracting me had been their plan all along.

I fumed, feeling every bit of the humiliation that washed over me as I thought about Axyl's fingers wrapped around mine.

"You can dunk me, Charlie," Duncan said with a smile. "I don't mind."

"Gag!" Iris said. "Good thing you're not obvious, Dunc."

"What?" Duncan asked innocently, though coloring slightly underneath his tan.

I shoved him out of the way to get to Brant.

"Are we dunking Brant?" Coleman yelled, swimming for us. "I want in on that."

"Hey!" Brant called. "Where's the love, bro?"

"Iris will protect you, Brant," I said with a hard smile.

Brant scowled and Iris blushed, but they moved toward each other, effectively choosing a side and encouraging the rest of us to choose sides also. Coleman retrieved the football and tossed it to Brant.

"I'm with Charlie," Duncan announced. Brant and Axyl frowned while Iris rolled her eyes.

"I'm with Charlie too," Axyl said, swimming to my side with a knowing smile. Apparently my throw from earlier spoke for itself.

"She does need the help," I heard Bailey tell Laney.

Unfortunately, Bailey chose our team, leaving Laney with Brant, Iris, Parker, and Coleman.

And even more unfortunate than that, I wouldn't have known Duncan was on my team if he hadn't announced it at the start. He spent more time finding creative ways to wrap his arms around me than passing the football to our team. He was more of a help to the opposing team in blocking me out than assisting our team.

Axyl, and even Brant playing for the other team, tried to run interference, but there was no dissuading Duncan. I was just getting ready to tell him to keep his hands off me when Laney claimed exhaustion and whined to get back on the boat. We were losing anyway. Bailey joined her, and the rest of us slowly straggled after.

Duncan swam past Axyl to beat him to the boat. As soon as he was on board, he turned and offered me a hand up. Axyl looked between Duncan's hand and me and frowned. Axyl pulled himself onto the boat after me.

"Ax, you can sit by me," Bailey invited, patting the seat beside her.

"You can sit between us," Laney told him. He hesitated, looking around the boat. I wondered what his hesitation was about. In the end, he wrapped his towel around his shoulders and slid in between them.

The sun was sinking in the sky, taking the warm temperatures with it. I wrapped my towel around my shoulders and slid over to put some space between Duncan and me.

"I brought a hoodie if you need to use it," Duncan offered.

"No, thanks," I replied, pulling my towel tighter around me. "I'm okay."

"Your lips are turning purple," he observed. "And your legs." He ran a finger down my bare thigh and I jumped.

Brant climbed on the boat just then and raised a brow at us.

I cringed inside. What must my exchange with Duncan have looked like?

"Watch yourself, man," Brant said to Duncan under his breath. "That's my sister."

Duncan inched away from me, a guilty look on his face.

Brant went to the other side of the boat to grab his towel, but he made sure Duncan knew he was watching us.

With Parker at the wheel, Coleman opened a cooler and tossed sodas to everyone. We settled back in our seats, content to allow the sun and wind to dry and warm us as we skipped over the water at breathtaking speeds. I ignored Duncan's repeated and unwelcome attempts to engage me in conversation as kindly as I could and instead watched how easily Brant and Axyl interacted with the others. Bits of their conversation and laughter carried on the wind to me. They were charismatic and funny. It was difficult to not fall under their spell like Bailey, Laney, and Iris were. When the sun threatened to call it a day and slipped toward the horizon, we were forced back to the dock.

Iris scooted into the space between Duncan and me and I breathed a sigh of relief. "Thanks for saving me a seat," she said to Duncan over his protests of there not being enough room. Then, turning to me, she said, "Coleman says we are heading to his cabin for s'mores. You coming?"

"I'll check with Brant," I told her, hopping up from the seat and moving to where Brant sat by Axyl, Bailey, and Laney. I was grateful for the excuse to move away from Duncan. His interest was making me squirm.

"What time did you tell Mom and Dad we'd be back?" I asked Brant softly.

"I didn't," he replied. "Why?"

"Iris said something about s'mores at Coleman's cabin. Are we going?"

Brant watched me, surprised. "You want to go?"

"I didn't say that," I told him, still keeping my voice low. "I wondered what the plan is."

Brant looked between me and the other end of the boat and frowned.

"You want to spend more time with Duncan?" he guessed. "Look at little Charlie having her first crush." He sniffed, pretending to wipe a tear from his eye. "My little sister is growing up." But he didn't sound happy about it.

"Who does Charles have a crush on?" Bailey interrupted, drawing Axyl's and Laney's attention our way also.

"No one," I huffed, widening my eyes at Brant to send the hint that he should either lower his voice or stop talking altogether. "We were talking about s'mores at Coleman's."

"Yes. You should come," Laney pouted, putting one arm through Axyl's and the other through Bailey's.

"How is Charlie growing up?" Axyl asked, apparently refusing to drop the subject. "She looks the same to me as she did earlier today."

My look at Brant was one part pleading and one part warning. If he dared say anything about Duncan...

"Charlie does look good today," Brant surprised me by replying. "She always does."

My cheeks warmed and my heart swelled at Brant's praise even though Axyl hadn't actually said I looked good. Brant was putting words in Axyl's mouth. And he *had* to keep talking...

"But she doesn't know it, so you'll have to compliment her a lot while you're here, Axyl. Maybe she'll believe it by the time you leave."

"That shouldn't be a problem," Duncan chimed in with a smile that made me cringe inside. Everyone groaned at his obvious crush. Now my cheeks were on fire and I glared at Brant. Just when I thought he'd take pity on me...

"Hey, Dunc," Parker said, "Give subtlety a try."

"What?" Duncan asked, holding his arms out. "How does Charlie not know she's hot?"

Coleman snorted and Iris giggled. Brant grinned at me like the Cheshire Cat.

My eyes darted around the boat, taking in the number of people who had a front row seat to my embarrassment before dropping my head and studying the pattern on my towel. I was seriously contemplating jumping ship and sinking to the bottom of the lake. I would make a good water nymph, I think.

"Charlie? Hot?" Bailey snorted, inserting herself into our conversation that was quickly moving from embarrassing to full fledged humiliating. "In that old swimming suit?" She laughed, holding out her sunglasses to Duncan. "Is the sunlight in your eyes?"

"I think the term is vintage, Bailey," Iris corrected. "Charlie has a hint of vintage to her that I can't figure out."

And I couldn't figure out why Iris would defend me, but I smiled my gratitude to her.

"Is that why Axyl is always 'bumping' into her?" came Bailey's snarky reply. Laney laughed like they shared an inside joke, but everyone else's eyes turned to Axyl. He shifted uncomfortably in his seat, the heightened coloring in his cheeks obvious even in the waning light.

My eyes narrowed. What she said wasn't true. He wasn't always bumping into me, was he? I mean, sure, he always seemed to be around. But then so was Brant. There weren't a heck of a lot of places to go around here. Axyl hadn't singled me out on purpose. In a premeditated way. No way.

"Because he won't have to play any guessing games with *me*," Bailey continued. "I'll tell him anything he wants to know."

Brant stood. "I'm suddenly feeling sick to my stomach," he said, covering his mouth with a hand like he was going to puke any second. "Good thing we're almost to the dock."

Axyl slipped his arm out of Laney's and stood also. Brant clapped him on the shoulder. And with a laugh that was somewhat strained, Axyl followed Brant up onto the bow and then to the dock, laughing like best friends about something.

"I'm secure enough in our relationship that him spending time with other girls doesn't make me jealous," Bailey informed Laney. "Especially when it's Charlie. Because we all know vintage is just a nice way of saying cheap and out of style…" Bailey laughed with an amused shake of her head as she sauntered away. With a toss of her hair, Laney followed in her wake.

"Harsh," Iris chided from the other side of the boat. "I don't think you've ever said how you know Bailey. Please tell me she isn't your friend."

I thought back to the first time we hopped on Coleman's boat. That's right. We'd probably only shared our names, not how the four of us were connected.

"She's my sister," I revealed dryly. We were so different from each other in every way. I could see how someone wouldn't make the connection that we were siblings

Iris paused in pulling a red hoodie over her silky head at my words. Her surprised "Oh" was more a quick intake of breath. "You know what they say. With friends like that…" She tugged her hoodie over her chest and stood and wrapped a towel around her slender waist.

I could only nod. I knew my sister and I were nothing even closely related to friends. It hadn't bothered me much before. It's just the way it had been of late. But to have an outsider pity me because of it felt…wrong…and sad.

"But Bailey's right, you know," Iris continued.

My brows pulled down and I peered at her in confusion. Had I misunderstood her vintage comment? Was she siding with Bailey?

She silently nodded in the direction Axyl and Brant went.

I shook my head, still unsure of her meaning.

"He keeps pretty close track of you."

"Oh," I laughed as her meaning finally became clear. "Brant's my brother, remember? He thinks it's his job to babysit me."

Now she laughed. "No. I know who Brant is." And the tone in her voice suggested she wouldn't mind knowing him better. "I'm talking about Axyl. He can't keep his eyes off you." She studied me through the fading light. "And why wouldn't he? You're vintage. It works for you. And that brat- your sister," she threw a thumb over her shoulder, "shouldn't make you think any different. She's jealous of you. And she has a right to be."

I watched Iris slide her feet into sandals and hop over the side of the boat, disappearing up the dock and into the darkening night like a beautiful wraith. I wanted to call her back- tell her to explain herself. The darkness must have been affecting her eyesight. Bailey wasn't jealous of anyone- least of all me. She had nothing to be jealous of.

I gathered my things and stepped carefully over the side of the boat to the shifting dock to find Brant. I'd had enough fun and sun for one day. And while I rarely turned down a good bonfire and sticky s'mores, I was finished interacting with people. My notebook was like a siren call in the night.

I found Brant standing in the bed of Coleman's red truck, surrounded by the group, telling some story that had everyone's undivided attention. I wasn't surprised. He could command a crowd. I waited until he had them laughing to interrupt.

"Brant," I called over the laughter. Iris turned and I nodded at Brant. She brushed his arm and leaned in to whisper in his ear. He turned and squatted down, leaning over the side of the truck to be closer to my level.

"I'm walking home," I told him.

"Not by yourself," he answered with a shake of his head. He raised his can of soda to his lips and took a sip, watching me over the rim of the can.

I rolled my eyes. "It's the lake, Brant. I'll be fine."

"It's dark, Charlie. The cabin is clear on the other side. I'll get *Duncan* to walk you home," he said. Though the laughter in his eyes negated any good feelings I should have had at his attempt at a compromise.

I quickly turned for the dirt road. "Bye!" I called over my shoulder. "See you at home."

A few goodbyes and Brant's displeased, *"Charlie..."*, followed me from the truck, but people didn't. I was relieved. How awkward would that have been if Brant had sent Duncan after me like I was some little kid who couldn't make it a quarter of a mile by herself? Well, a quarter of a mile on my side of the lake. From the other side, it was double the distance, but I knew this lake like the back of my hand.

When I heard gravel crunching behind me a ways down the road, I growled that Brant had sent someone to follow me back after all, but when I turned my head to look over my shoulder, the figure walking behind me wasn't Duncan. Too short and bulky for Duncan. I could make out that much in the fading light. Though it was a male. It wasn't even Brant. Or Axyl. I picked up my pace and so did the person walking behind me. I kicked it up another notch until I was almost jogging.

"Hey! Hold up," a male voice called behind me. The quickened footsteps and ragged breathing told me the man was jogging now too. His voice was familiar, but I couldn't place it and tiny tentacles of fear wriggled close to my heart.

"Sorry," I returned. "I have somewhere I need to be and I'm late." I was almost running now.

I didn't want to lead whoever it was to our cabin, so I cut through the neighbor's yard and came up the far side of our cabin. I hoped the few trees between their cabin and ours, added to my frantic pace, put enough distance between me and the man that he didn't see where I went.

I came around the corner of our cabin and skidded to a stop, barely keeping my balance in the gravel, when a form stepped from the shadows in front of me and two strong hands gripped my arms just below the shoulders. I yanked back with a cry.

"Charlie! It's me. Axyl."

My shoulders slumped in relief and I stopped struggling. "Axyl," I panted. "What are you doing?" I was grateful for the dark so he couldn't see the crazed look in my eyes.

"What are *you* doing?" he asked. "Why are you coming from that direction? The lake is that way." He pointed over his shoulder.

I looked in the direction he pointed and then scanned the area, my senses on alert for anyone else. The darkness wasn't my friend right now. Who knew what lurked in the shadows.

"Are Bailey and Brant behind you?"

"They said they'd come in a while."

"You didn't want s'mores?"

I could barely make out his shrug in the dark.

"It's been a long day."

I nodded my understanding. It *had* been a long day in the sun. I was ready for a shower and my hoodie.

I turned and started up the steps. Axyl's footsteps followed after me.

"I'm undefeated at Uno," he said. My head spun at his change of topic and I frowned in confusion. "Wanna see if you can break my record?"

I felt my lips lift into a smile. "I am also undefeated at Uno," I informed him. His white teeth shone bright in the moonlight as a grin slowly split his lips. He opened the door for me and I glanced over my shoulder into the darkness one last time before going inside to get the Uno cards.

Chapter 9

"I'm going hiking in the morning," Brant told me over roasted marshmallows the next night.

Apparently things had gone so well the night before with Coleman and the Crew that Brant invited them to our cabin tonight for a campfire. Mom and Kristen were at the picnic table making sure to keep the s'more supplies well stocked. Dad and Matt manned the fire.

"You wanna come with me?" Brant asked. "I was thinking of inviting Axyl too."

We both peered across the campfire at Axyl. His mallow was on fire and he shoved it in Bailey's face so she could blow it out for him. Bailey squirmed and squealed, so he brought it as close to his face as he could with it being on the end of a long stick and blew. The marshmallow wasn't salvageable, so he jabbed it into the fire and watched it bubble and grow until it fell off the stick into the coals.

"Heads up," Brant called to Axyl, lobbing another marshmallow through the air to him. Axyl easily caught it and slid it onto his stick.

"Thanks, man," Axyl called back to Brant.

"No worries," Brant said, holding up the open bag of marshmallows he was holding. "I have to sit over here by Charlie. She roasts mallows worse than you."

Axyl grinned at me. "I just burned mine to make her feel better."

He seemed more relaxed around me since our Uno tournament the previous night. Or maybe I was more relaxed around him…I remained undefeated, winning eight out of ten games. Even Brant and all his talk wasn't enough to damage my winning streak.

Bailey had really missed out when she'd decided to forego the games to give herself a manicure instead.

I shot him a mock glare and he and Brant laughed.

"I could roast one for you, Charlie," Duncan said.

"That's okay," I replied, groaning inside. "But thanks."

Duncan beamed at me and went back to his conversation with Parker.

Axyl snorted at the exchange then lifted his stick out of the coals and held it up for my inspection. "Look at this perfect, golden mallow," he bragged, practically caressing his marshmallow. "You wish you were as good as me."

"You going to eat it, or take it on a date?" I asked.

Brant let out a surprised laugh. "Good one, Charlie."

I watched as Axyl went to the table to slide his sticky, golden brown and white blob onto a graham. He threw on a few rectangles of chocolate, another square of cracker, and brought it to his mouth, declaring it delicious. Then I scooted across the log into Brant as Axyl came our way and sat down next to me.

Brant elbowed me in the ribs. "Sheesh, Charlie. He doesn't need that much room. Scoot over."

"Did Charlie call me fat?" Axyl asked, affronted, then tore into his s'more with another huge bite.

"No!"

Axyl elbowed me good naturedly.

"I'm going hiking in the morning," Brant told Axyl. "You coming?"

Axyl shrugged then nodded. "Sure. Thanks."

I flashed Brant an annoyed look. He raised a brow, but said nothing. I had been looking forward to spending some time alone with Brant without anyone else tagging along. Even if Axyl was growing on me.

"Hey, Brant!" Dad called. "Where's the Uke?"

Brant turned and produced a Ukulele from the ground behind the log we were sitting on and strummed it, loosening or tightening the strings to tune.

"*Ghost Riders*," Dad requested.

"Charlie wants *Kumbaya*," Axyl said, nudging me with his elbow. I elbowed him back. Hard. He laughed.

Brant laughed. "Whoa. One at a time."

He played a brief intro for *Ghost Riders* and nodded to bring everyone in.

We'd done this for as many years as I could remember, so my family sang out. Singing was one thing Bailey liked to do, so I wasn't as shocked as I normally would have been when she smiled across the fire at me.

Memories of summer's past ran through my mind. I was startled to remember that there had actually been times when Bailey and I had gotten along pretty well.

At one point, Axyl leaned in and said, "You're not too bad, Charlie."

I felt the blush creep up my face and wished the fire hadn't died down so I had something to blame it on. Thank heaven the darkness would hide the worst of it.

"Now *Kumbaya*, for Charlie," Brant said with a wink in my direction.

"Funny, Brant," I muttered.

As if they'd planned it, Brant and Axyl scooted into me, sandwiching me between them and swaying back and forth to *Kumbaya*. I finally gave in and pushed back with exaggerated sways to the left and right. Axyl threw an arm over my shoulders to pull me down and we ended up laughing more than singing. That's all it took to erase the smile off Bailey's face and the sisterly bond between us shattered, breathing ice across the fire at me.

After a few more song requests, Dad and Matt doused the fire and the moms gathered up the snacks. Bailey said goodbye to Laney then complained she was cold and dragged Axyl toward the house, hugging his arm close for warmth.

Duncan watched me from across the fire pit with something like longing in his eyes. I didn't want to encourage him, though, so when Iris glanced in my direction, I waved her over, although I knew she was watching Brant and not me.

"Thanks for inviting us, Brant," Iris said with a shy smile.

Brant looked uncomfortable, but smiled in return. "No problem. We'll have to get together again in a few days. Not just...With everyone. I mean...the whole group."

I bit my lip to keep from laughing at how he tripped over his words. So he wasn't invincible. Stick a pretty girl in front of him and he was almost as awkward as I am. How cute.

Iris giggled and blushed. "I'll talk to everyone," she promised. "And you..." she said, putting a hand on my arm and leaning closer, lowering her voice.

"Me?" I asked.

"You and your green eyes."

Those eyes, clearly *not* green, narrowed in confusion.

"My eyes are hazel," I told her.

"Well, that hoodie makes them look dark green. You should wear that color more often. Axyl couldn't stay away. You had Bailey and Duncan shooting daggers across the fire." She laughed like that would be funny. "Everyone could see you were into each other."

I sucked in a ragged breath. Into each other? Everyone? Even Axyl? No!

"I don't think so," I disagreed. "That's not what was happening."

"That's what it looked like to me. See you guys later." She squeezed my arm and gave Brant one more flirtatious smile before jogging to catch up with Laney and Parker.

Duncan turned back when she joined them and caught my eye. "Text me," he mouthed as he mimed holding a phone and pushing keys with his thumbs.

Brant groaned something that sounded like *loser* and we walked up the stone path to the cabin in silence. I didn't know where Brant's thoughts were, but Iris' words replayed in my mind, flooding me with embarrassment all over again. Had I been so obvious? Had I acted like Bailey, throwing myself at Axyl, fake laughing and flirting like a pro? I wanted to shrivel up and die from humiliation. The shame that wouldn't let up firmed my resolve that Axyl couldn't go on that hike with us in the morning.

"Please don't let Axyl come on the hike tomorrow, Brant," I begged, keeping my voice low. "I just want it to be you and me."

"I already invited him, Charlie. I can't say, 'Axyl, about that hike tomorrow...Just kidding. I don't want you to come after all.' Why don't you like him?" Brant asked.

I hung my head and studied the rock path we walked on. "I'm just a huge joke to him," I confessed. "He laughs at me all the time."

"I laugh at you all the time and you don't hate me," he pointed out.

"*Much,*" I replied. "I don't hate you much."

Brant feigned shock and hurt. "Charlie is joking?! I don't believe it." He reached out and knocked on my head with the back of a knuckle. "Will the real Charlie please come out?"

I swatted his hand away with a laugh. "I'm not that sterile, am I?"

"You're not the life of the party either."

I frowned. "I know. But what's wrong with being quiet...reserved? Just because I don't say anything doesn't mean I'm not happy. And just because someone jokes around all the time doesn't mean they *are*."

"You're right. It's just so quiet around the house sometimes." He rolled his eyes. "Besides Bailey. But who wants to listen to her drama all the time? Some intelligent conversation would be nice."

"What makes you think my conversation would be intelligent?"

"Wow! You are on one tonight." He sounded pleased and that made me happy. "But back to Axyl. Why aren't you giving him a chance? I mean, Bailey laughs at you all the time and you don't treat her like you treat him." He nudged me with an arm. "You played Uno with him last night and it didn't look too painful."

He paused for a moment on the path, thinking. Then his eyes lit up like someone had flipped a switch in his brain. "You like him."

"What?" I asked, mortified.

"You liiiike him," he teased.

"No I don't." But I was sure my flaming face told the real story.

"You do," Brant crowed. "You have a crush on the college guy." He laughed and shook his head. "Poor Duncan."

I snorted at the thought of me and Duncan, but Brant continued, "Axyl Stewart. I mean, what's not to crush on? Look at him. If I was a girl, I'd think he was hot."

I *had* looked at him. That was part of the problem. The other part of the problem was that he seemed to be everywhere I was. I liked the attention. It was new and flattering. But I couldn't tell Brant that. No way!

"You think he's hot?" I asked, amused. "I'll be sure to let him know. Maybe I'll ditch the hike. You two could go. Just the two of you. I'll try to keep Bailey away." I finished that last part in a mutter, glancing up the path to the cabin where Bailey had dragged Axyl moments before. If Axyl was everywhere, Bailey was everywhere Axyl was.

"Bailey does seem to be crushing pretty hard," Brant agreed. "But when doesn't she?"

I nodded. True.

"So," he continued, "Bailey's behavior is normal for Bailey. It's Charlie's behavior I'm interested in." He'd pulled out his clinical voice and I knew he was watching me closely.

"Save the questioning, Freud. There's nothing here worth delving into."

"Ah, but I think there is." He circled me like a pesky mosquito, arms folded. "We've already established that you like him."

I shoved him. "No we haven't."

He continued as if I hadn't spoken. "*How much* do you like him? *That* is the question. And what will I do about it?"

My eyes widened. "You won't *do* anything, Brantley, because there is nothing *to* do."

"It's Brantley, is it?" His eyes glowed with triumph.

Shoot. I'd used his full first name. That was the biggest tell of all.

"So let's go over what we know-"

I clapped my hand over his mouth. "No. Let's not." I stood on tip-toe and glared up into his eyes. "And don't say anything about this to anyone," I hissed.

Brant laughed. "I ain't afraid of you. No, ma'am," he drawled. "I already invited him. I'm not going to uninvite him."

I frowned and stomped my foot. "Dang it."

We started up the path again.

"I guess I won't go," I said.

"No. You have to go too. The three of us are going." He held up a hand to stop my protests and sprinted to the cabin. "See you bright and early," he called over his shoulder.

If I hadn't been so flustered about my transparent feelings for Axyl, I would have turned the tables on Brant and teased him about Iris. He could use a good mocking about a girl. Maybe it would humble him a little.

•••••

The next morning, I pulled a hoodie over my head and threw my hair up into a messy bun. I swiped a granola bar from the kitchen cupboard and a water bottle from the fridge on my way out the door.

Brant and Axyl were waiting on the front porch. They both looked up when I opened the door.

"'Bout time," Brant grouched. "I was about to go get you."

"Morning, Charlie," Axyl said with a half smile. "I didn't know you were tagging along."

"Brant's afraid of snakes," I informed him, bouncing down the stairs. I had to get moving or my legs would fall off in the brisk morning air. They were covered in goosebumps, but I knew from experience that I'd be glad I'd worn shorts in an hour when the sun heated things up.

Except for the early bird or occasional croak from a frog, we walked silently down to the lake and boarded the kayaks. Brant nodded to me to lead out. I dug into the sleepy lake with a strong paddle. My body responded and I smiled and looked around me. The air felt cleaner and the day felt full of promise. I patted my notebook nestled in my hoodie pouch. My fingers itched to get the wonders around me down on paper. My mind whirled with the words that spun around like a tornado looking for a place to land.

"I can see why Charlie likes it here," Axyl said, pulling me out of my reverie.

I glanced at him out of the corner of my eye, but otherwise gave no indication that I'd heard him.

"It's okay, I guess," Brant agreed, grinning at me. Guess there was no fooling him. I stuck my tongue out at him and his grin broadened.

"What would you write in your notebook about this, Charlie?" Axyl asked.

I flushed in embarrassment. "About what?" I asked.

He swirled his paddle in the air in a circular motion encompassing the lake and surrounding mountains. "About this morning on the lake, of course. The majestic mountains. The chill in the air. The smell of sage on the crisp breeze."

Brant laughed. "You sound like Charlie. Majestic…" He scoffed with a shake of his head.

Axyl gave an embarrassed chuckle. "Just trying to speak her language."

So even my words were a joke to him. They were the only thing I had that were my own. His making light of them was the exact reason I didn't share with others.

I ignored him and Brant and paddled faster to put some distance between us.

"What did I say?" I heard Axyl question.

"Let her go," was Brant's reply.

Brant and Axyl fell behind and I was gratefully left to myself. Who needed them? Who needed anyone? I was always better off by myself.

I arrived at the area where we usually ditch the kayaks for the hiking trail and scraped up onto the small piece of rocky shoreline. I clumsily got to my feet and pulled the kayak farther onto the bank to keep it from floating away. It would be a long walk back if my kayak wandered away without me! Seconds later, Brant and Axyl's kayaks scraped in behind me. They must have really dug in to catch up. I had put good distance between us.

"Did you miss us?" Brant asked, easily hefting his kayak up the bank into the long grass and sage brush.

"Not really," I responded. "You talk too much."

"That's right," Axyl chimed in. "Charlie likes her solitude." I watched him pull a small pack onto his back and wondered at his words. I could never tell if he was restating facts or making fun.

I turned without a word and started up the trail.

"Where's the fire?" Brant called.

"The day's wasting while I wait for you," I hollered over my shoulder. "It will be hot soon."

Brant's mutterings were swallowed up in the crunching of my shoes on the dusty trail. I admired the orange butterflies and silvery dragonflies that flitted about, landing only momentarily because there was so much to explore that they couldn't spend excess time on any one plant. Purple and yellow wildflowers were sprinkled across the mountainside like heaven had tossed them from above, letting them land where they may. I sighed in contentment. God sure knew what He was doing when He painted this mountain scene.

About a mile up the trail, I stopped for a drink. I also shed my hoodie, tying it around my waist. I stretched my arms over my head and shook my hands out at my sides. I looked behind me and was surprised to see Brant coming up fast.

"What's the matter with you?" he demanded, taking a long sip of his water. Well, that was the question, wasn't it? Whenever Axyl was around, I felt jumbled up inside. I wasn't myself. "You're acting like a spoiled brat."

"I'm acting like a spoiled brat?" I asked, my brows rising in surprise.

"Yes. Axyl was only trying to engage you in conversation back in the water and you got all mad and paddled off. And when we caught up, you ditched us. What's that about?"

"He wasn't trying to engage me in conversation," I argued. "He was making fun of me. Just like you and Bailey make fun of me. I am just a big joke to all of you."

"Oh, come off it, Charlie." Brant ground out. "You know that's not true. I can't speak for Bailey, but I tease you to keep you from taking yourself so seriously. That's all."

I peered at him closely, studying him for sincerity.

"Fine," I conceded. "But I don't have to like Axyl. Have you seen him? He's exactly like Bailey and I only need one Bailey in my life. One is one too many," I muttered under my breath.

Brant's brows rose. "Axyl? Just like Bailey? You mean our self-absorbed, princess little sister, Bailey?"

"Yes, Brant. How many Bailey's do you know?"

Brant chuckled humorlessly. "Don't take this the wrong way, Charlie, but get over yourself." I sucked in an enraged breath as his words struck my pride with a fierce blow, but Brant raised a hand and continued over me. "Axyl is nothing like Bailey. How can you not see that? He may be a bit of a pretty boy, but that ends with his trendy haircut and designer t-shirts. You've seen how he's repeatedly tried to be your friend since he got here. And all you've done is push him away with your snark and bad attitude." My shoulders sagged and my eyes stared holes in the trail with each of Brant's words. "He's not like Bailey, Charlie. If you'd give him a chance you would see that."

He leaned down slightly to see up into my face. "You can either try to make friends with Axyl and have a great day with us or you can go off and have your pity party like you tend to do. I can tell you from personal experience, it's more fun hanging with Axyl and me." He bumped my shoulder with his own playfully, attempting to fun me out of my wounded silence. "You know I'm the life of any party. And Axyl's not half bad either."

"I heard that," Axyl hollered from somewhere to our right. "Come on, Charlie. Brant's not that bad. Come be with us." He pushed past us and continued up the trail.

Brant nudged me again. "See? Come on, Charlie. Be the person I know you are and quit sulking." He gave me a light shove, urging me ahead of him, and I reluctantly stumbled after Axyl.

"One year at scout camp," Axyl began, "we told the younger boys that we were in bear country and they needed to be careful, at night especially, or the bears would creep out and carry the boys off in their sleep.

"We'd wait up until we heard them snoring, then we'd sneak out of our tents and scare them a little." He chuckled. "We'd make moaning and snorting noises, shake and scratch at their tents...Freaked them right out." He and Brant laughed together.

Though I hated to admit it, I was getting caught up in his story and was glad when he continued. "But one night, after they'd figured out it was us, they tried to get us back. They were stomping around outside our tent, being so noisy that there was no question it was humans not bears. I crawled out of my sleeping bag and threw open the tent flap, ready to call them on their terrible attempt at scaring us. I was pretty surprised when I was face to face with a legit black bear."

"No way," Brant argued in disbelief.

Axyl stopped and turned to us.

"No joke," he insisted. "It was a black bear. I fell back into the tent, stuttering, 'Bear. Bear.' I sounded like an idiot." He laughed at himself. "I fumbled around for my can of bear spray, about peeing my pants the whole time. The other guys in my tent finally woke up, but by then, the bear had lost interest and wandered off. The guys didn't believe me."

"I don't believe you," Brant said with a laugh. I was skeptical myself.

"I'm being serious," Axyl said, raising three fingers in the scout sign. "Honest." He turned back and started up the trail again. "Scared me to death."

"Why is it that whenever I hear about something bad happening during the summer, a group of boy scouts is involved?" I asked.

"'Cause guys are stupid," Axyl said with a snort. "And when you put a group of us together, the IQ level goes down significantly."

Brant laughed. "Way down. But we have fun." He held up a fist and Axyl reached over my head to bump it with his own.

"I've never understood the fun of swamping canoes, getting lost on hikes for weeks, or sitting in glacier water just to see if I can."

Brant and Axyl shared a smile.

"That's the fun of it," Brant said.

I shook my head. "I guess that's why women live longer than men."

"That's exactly why," Axyl chuckled.

Revelation...I liked his laugh. When it wasn't aimed at me, it made me want to smile. And I liked the fact that he didn't take himself too seriously. He could laugh at himself right along with everyone else. Did that make the teasing less hurtful? I'd never been able to laugh at myself very well.

I hiked along between the two men, listening to their stories and finding myself laughing along with them. Brant was right. Axyl wasn't bad. But why become friends, let him in, when I'd never see him again?

Despite my resolve, when he carried my kayak to the shore and held it so I could get in, when he teasingly offered to splash me with lake water to help me cool off, and when he said something funny that had Brant laughing so hard he almost capsized his kayak, I found myself arguing that letting him in a bit wouldn't hurt anything.

"There's a bat cave up the road a ways," I informed Axyl later that day. We'd been back from the hike for hours. After cooling off in the lake for a bit, I was ready for more exploring.

"You know Batman?" he asked with a smirk.

"Ha, ha," I deadpanned. "No. A cave where bats live. Sonar. Guano."

"Sure. I'm up for studying bat poop," he replied, falling into step beside me.

"You coming, Brant?" I asked over my shoulder.

"No," he replied, waving us on without looking up from his phone.

"Iris," Axyl explained.

"Oh," I mouthed, then smiled. I liked Iris and I thought it was cute that Brant did too.

We left the lake and hiked up the steep mountainside to a cave. It wasn't very big and it smelled awful.

Axyl cringed and shook his head. "What's that smell?"

I extended my arm to take in the cave. "The bat poop," I told him proudly. I squatted down to look at the poop painting the cave floor. "It's kind of cool."

Axyl watched me, not saying anything.

"What?" I asked, turning my face up to meet his eyes.

"Nothing," he said with a small smile tugging at the corners of his mouth.

I frowned. It was a stupid idea to show him the cave. Who wanted to see bat poop? I squirmed inside when I thought of what a loser he probably thought I was.

Laugh with him, I reminded myself. *He doesn't take life too seriously.*

"Look up there," I said, standing and pointing above our heads at the chimney-like way the cave rose above us to the cloudless blue sky. "That's how they get in and out." I stepped around him and led the way back out of the cave. "There's another cave up here," I said, pointing as I stepped around a clump of sagebrush and began zigzagging my way upward. Before long, I paused to catch my breath at the mouth of a shallow cave that water, wind, and time had carved out of rock. Though I could stand upright in the cave, I sat down at the opening, perching at the edge of the ledge with my feet dangling over.

Axyl took a seat beside me and gazed out across the valley, taking in the neat row of cabins just below us and the lake and mountains beyond. Reds and browns of the cliffs melting into neutrals of man's mark, spreading out to blues of the water and then browns and reds of the mountains reaching for the blues of the sky. They all blended together and circled around to meet up with us again. We were just a small part of the bigger picture.

"This is a great place," he said. "Bat poop and all."

I looked at him out of the corner of my eye. He seemed serious.

"You're going to be a senior, right?" he asked, picking up a rock and lobbing it through the air. We watched it hit the ground below us and bounce before rolling down to the road.

"Yeah."

"What do you want to do after high school?"

"I'm going to do a humanitarian trip in Mexico."

His eyes widened and he turned them on me. "Really? That's cool. What will you do?"

"Help build a school," I replied. "And take care of kids in an orphanage."

He nodded his head and looked out at the lake again.

"Then what?" he asked.

"College. A job." I shrugged.

"You sound so excited about it," he said wryly.

I took a deep breath before admitting, "I guess I have a hard time with change." I shrugged, trying to make my words sound less heavy. "Brant's leaving for school in the fall and I hate it."

"You two seem close."

I nodded. "He's my best friend." I peered up at him through my lashes. "I don't know if you know this about me, but I have a hard time making friends."

His lips threatened to turn up into a smile, but he scoffed instead. "No way! Charlie the Unapproachable can't make friends?"

"Go ahead and laugh." He would anyway. "Brant lets me have my space. But then he gets in my face and makes me think." I frowned. "It's annoying how he can tease me out of a bad mood. He...he understands me." My voice caught on the last word, but I blinked rapidly to keep the tears back. I wouldn't cry and give Axyl one more thing to laugh at.

"It would be cool to have someone like that around all the time," Axyl said, surprising me. "You're lucky."

"I won't have anyone when he leaves. Things will change. He won't be the same when he comes home to visit."

Axyl nodded. "Probably. But that's a good thing."

I shook my head back and forth vigorously, disagreeing. "I hate change." Even thinking about the word made my breaths come faster. Mutant butterflies filled my chest and pressed against my ribs to get out. I rubbed a hand there, forcing them back.

"Is that an eagle?" Axyl asked, pointing at a blot in the sky in the distance.

I squinted and looked where he was pointing. "I don't see anything," I said, shaking my head. "Though I wouldn't be surprised. There are eagles all over here. Brant and I even saw a bobcat perched on a cliff one canyon over a few years ago."

"Hm," was his nonchalant reply. "I could have sworn I saw something."

I watched him for a minute as he purposely avoided my gaze. My eyes widened as it hit me that he had kept me from having a melt down by taking my mind off it just like Brant always did. Now my heart rate sped up for a different reason entirely. I suddenly noticed the lack of space between us and how if I leaned slightly our arms would be touching from shoulder to elbow. My stomach swirled and I stared off at the horizon hoping my face wasn't red.

"Brant will change," Axyl said softly, glancing down at me. "But you will too. And you will have an excuse to spend more time with him when he comes around so you can figure out how you both have changed."

I nodded slowly. "I guess so."

Axyl bumped me with his arm. "Go ahead and tell me how wise I am. I can take it."

I rolled my eyes. "Careful, or I'll have to start calling you Brant."

We sat in silence, watching the valley below. A skier wiped out on the water and a boat lazily turned and went to pick him up. A couple in a paddle boat apparently couldn't get the hang of pedaling because the boat was turning in circles, going nowhere. The cry of an eagle pierced the air and had Axyl and me looking at each other with mutual knowing grins.

"And you won't be completely alone," Axyl said, picking up the conversation again. "You have your sister."

A short laugh burst from me. "Bailey and I are not the best of friends." That was putting it mildly, but he didn't need to know all the drama that was my precarious relationship with my younger sibling.

I squirmed a little, embarrassed at my internal conflict. I wanted to reciprocate and ask him more about himself, but maybe he liked quiet. Maybe he was bored and ready to head back down to the cabin.

Just ask him, I told myself. *Don't be nosy*, I argued. *He asked you about your plans. What's the difference?*

I took a deep breath. "What are you doing in the fall?" I asked in a rush.

If he was bothered by the question, he didn't show it. "College. Texas Tech."

"Are you excited?"

He grinned over at me. "Yeah. Can't wait." And I could tell by his smile that did weird things to my stomach that he was as excited about leaving as Brant was. My gaze flitted over his handsome face and down to his expensive clothes. I was not in his league in any way, I reminded myself as I looked at my worn cutoffs and faded tee.

I thought of all the beautiful girls he'd meet at college and my heart sank. But of course he'd meet someone, many someones, maybe. He was as friendly and outgoing as Brant. Why would he remember a plain, unapproachable nobody like me? I was still in high school. Young, immature. Not able to compete with all the sophisticated, fun girls at Texas Tech. Besides, we didn't even really know each other and would never see each other again.

Well, if we wouldn't see each other again, I reasoned, why not learn all I could about him while I had the chance. If he thought I was like a pesky little sister with all my questions, he'd only have to put up with me for a few more days and then I'd be nothing more than an annoying memory. Not even that. An unremarkable blip on the timeline in the story of his life.

I gulped and asked, "Do you know what you want to be when you grow up?"

"A web developer," he replied.

"Sounds interesting and...maybe a little boring."

"Boring?" he laughed in surprise. "No way!"

I peered up at him with one eye squinted. "So you're super smart, huh?"

"Not any smarter than you with your huge vocabulary and straight A's."

"You don't know if I get straight A's."

"That's all Bailey talks about is how her sister is so smart and doesn't even have to work to get a 4.0."

"I'll bet you she didn't say smart," I objected. *Nerd* was more like it.

"Brant is proud of you," Axyl said.

"What about you? No brothers or sisters who will miss you when you leave?" I asked.

Axyl nodded. "Two older brothers. But they aren't at home anymore. Just me. One's married and the other is in the army."

I was a little jealous of his solitude. "How has that been being the only one at home?"

"Lonely," he admitted. "But it's not so bad. I don't have to compete for my parent's attention. I don't have to live in anyone's shadow anymore. I don't have to share a bedroom."

I thought of Bailey and me in the cabin loft with limited privacy and her lack of respect for my things and made a noise of agreement. "Now that is something I could get used to."

"But I also don't have anyone to argue with, take the blame for me, or talk to when Dad and Mom aren't being fair."

"Yeah," I said quietly. "I guess there is that."

"You're pretty lu-"

"Hey, you two!" Kristen hollered up the mountain at us. Our gazes snapped to the valley floor. We couldn't hear her clearly, but we got the point as she mimed bringing a utensil to her mouth. "Dinner's ready."

I looked around and noticed the sun was in a different position than when we first hiked up the mountain.

"I didn't realize so much time had passed," Axyl said, mirroring my thoughts.

I jumped to my feet and dusted myself off. "Me either," I replied.

"Thanks for talking," Axyl said, watching me with a small smile.

"Uh, yeah. Sure," I stammered. And I could talk to him. I felt like he listened and was actually interested in what I had to say. My innermost thoughts didn't seem to make him look at me like the idiot I felt I was all the time.

"Race you to the bottom," he said, picking up the pace, half sliding, half falling down the mountainside.

"I'll just meet you down there," I called after him. "I'd like to live to eat dinner."

"Where's the fun in that?" he asked over his shoulder.

Chapter 10

Dark clouds moved swiftly across the sky, pulling a shroud over the brilliant blue day the next afternoon. I looked up just as lightning cut a jagged line through the pall on the other side of the lake, filling the waterlogged air with brief, instant light. I immediately began counting, grinning when thunder answered in a deep, rumbly voice in the distance. Six miles away.

"Storm's coming," Brant announced, peering into the darkening sky.

It had become kind of an unspoken thing that we met at the lake every afternoon. Sometimes with Coleman and the Crew, sometimes without. I couldn't decide whether I liked it more with the whole big group so I could observe from the periphery or with just the four of us so I had more of a chance to get to know Axyl one on one. Either scenario had Bailey boldly vying for his attention so it shouldn't have really mattered one way or the other. But it looked like the rain would ruin any more time at the lake today.

With my notebook in hand and my towel thrown over one shoulder, I called a quick goodbye to Bailey, Axyl, and Brant, and picked up the pace to make it in time. Gravel crunched beneath my hurried flip flops making their popping sound staccato against my heels. I jogged up the steps and threw open the cabin door and took the stairs to the loft two at a time, racing across the room to my bed and snatching the quilt off. I hustled back out to the porch, wrapped the blanket securely around myself and dropped into one of the deck chairs. I sat forward, eagerly watching the storm blow over the mountains and the lake, coming at me like waves rolling across the sea and onto the shore, tickling my toes and making me suck in a delighted breath.

"You're so weird," Bailey grumbled, flinging the door open and hurrying inside to get out of the rain.

Brant leaned against the porch railing to finish typing out a text and then ducked into the cabin with a secretive smile on his face.

"So how do we do this?" Axyl asked, taking a seat in the vacant chair next to me and eyeing me expectantly.

My brows tugged down in confusion and I dragged my eyes away from the storm. "How do we do what?"

"Wait out a storm," he said, his eyes widening like the answer should have been obvious. "You look like you've done this before, with the blanket and stuff. So how do we do it?"

I sat back stunned. "You've never listened to a rainstorm?"

Axyl chuckled. "Why would I do that?"

I frowned, the storm momentarily forgotten. Of course he'd never watched a rainstorm. Like Bailey, he thought I was a couple logs short of a cabin. It was like he hung around me just to see what stupid thing I would do next so he could laugh about it. But instead of taking offense, I decided to teach him the proper way to experience a downpour. If he made light of it, that was his loss.

"You missed the exciting build up with the lightning and thunder," I told him. "But there's nothing we can do about that. Do you get cold easily? You'll need a blanket if you do." I nodded behind us at the cabin. "The key is to be as cozy as possible so the cold doesn't force you inside prematurely."

Axyl shoved his hands into the kangaroo pouch on his hoodie and shook his head. "I'm good."

I nodded.

"Storms in the mountains come on fast," I told him. "And they can pass just as quickly. So you need to get into place as soon as possible or it could be over before you experience it."

He nodded his understanding, peering past the covered porch at the steadily falling rain.

"You haven't missed it all," I assured him.

"Whew!" he blew out a breath then grinned at me.

I rolled my eyes, but a smile tugged at my lips.

"What's next?" he asked.

"You have to be still," I said softly.

He shifted in his seat. "Like how still?" he asked at normal volume.

Whoa. Whoa. Too loud.

"More still than that," I muttered. To which he grinned. "Listen to the sound the rain makes on the roof. Pay attention to how the colors around you become more vibrant even as they get blurry like a watercolor painting."

I watched him pretend to be hyper aware of his surroundings- taking it all in with a serious, studious expression that you'd use if you were admiring fine artwork in a museum. He glanced at me out of the corner of his eye, and when he knew I was watching, he couldn't suppress another grin. But it didn't seem like he was laughing *at* me this time. Instead, it appeared that he was trying to get me to laugh at him. "I think I'm getting the hang of this," he told me.

I shook my head. What a goof.

"Now what?" he asked.

"Which direction is the wind blowing?"

He stuck a finger into his mouth and pulled it out with a pop before holding it up to catch the breeze.

I ignored him and asked, "What does the air smell like?"

He leaned toward me and made a big deal of sniffing. I shoved him away with a hand on his face. "Not me!" As if he didn't know.

He chuckled. "Fine. Kind of like wet flowers and dirt." I started to nod, but he continued, "And laundry detergent and coconut."

I shifted uncomfortably while he bit back a smirk.

"Wet flowers and dirt," I repeated pointedly. "Smells good, huh?"

He tipped his head and regarded me before staring out into the rain. "I've never thought about it before, but I guess it is a comforting smell."

I nodded, satisfied with his answer.

"It's kind of cool the way everything is getting wet and you can feel the water in the air, but you aren't getting wet," he commented.

I watched him for signs of teasing, but his steady gaze met mine and I saw sincerity there. A slow smile spread across my face. He got it! And I was certain my genuine smile broadcasted my pleasure.

He flashed me an answering smile and my grin grew. I knew I looked like a fool, but I couldn't wipe the smile off my face even though I felt it heating up in embarrassment.

Axyl cleared his throat and looked back out at the rain making dents in the puddles on the gravel road and shivered. "We aren't wet," he repeated, "but I'm getting cold!" He threw his hood over his head and stood slightly from his chair, sliding it across the few feet separating us. "Share the blanket, Charlie."

The smile left my mouth and I pulled back, holding the blanket tightly to my chest. "Get your own blanket," I replied. "I told you."

Axyl's eyes sparkled and I knew I'd cave if he looked at me like that much longer. He leaned forward and grasped the edge of the quilt. "Share the blanket, Charlie," he murmured, giving it a soft tug.

My mouth opened to refuse him, but only a squeak came out.

I watched helplessly as he went to his feet, held out his hands for mine, shaking them insistently when I resisted. Finally, I sighed and placed my hands in his, noticing how they were as much of a contradiction as he was- rough and gentle at the same time. I sucked in a breath as his warm fingers tightened around my cold ones and he pulled me up. The blanket fell away and he caught it before it puddled on the deck at our feet. He shook the blanket out and nodded at my chair.

"Have a seat," he said. He dropped one half of the blanket onto my lap before sitting down in his chair. He arranged the blanket over himself, checking to make sure I still had enough to cover me. He tucked his edge under himself and shoved his hands back into his kangaroo pouch. He extended his legs out in front of him, crossed at the ankles, and sighed.

"Perfect," he stated, glancing over at me with a satisfied smile. "Right?"

I folded my legs under me and pulled the blanket up to my chin, glancing at him out of the corner of my eye. "It's good."

I saw his grin spread and bit my cheek to keep my face blank, but lost the battle as he settled deeper into his chair and silently sat and watched the rain.

"Perfect," he whispered.

We watched the rain in companionable silence for a few minutes, then Axyl straightened in his chair and threw me a mischievous grin.

"It has been brought to my attention that I need to expand my horizons," he began.

"Yeah? How so?"

"I've decided that I am going to become a part-time poet."

I raised a brow. "A part-time...poet?" My eyes broadcasted my skepticism.

"A part-time poet," he repeated, attempting to look serious, and not in the least put off by my doubt. "This rain is inspiring. And I'm no expert, but this is going to be a good one."

I knew my expression was bogged down in amused disbelief.

"Really," he insisted. "Just because you're a professional poet doesn't mean you need to be a snob."

"Sno-" I began, my voice rising. But Axyl raised a hand, demanding silence.

"I call it...*Ode to Rainstorms*," he said with a hand in the air emphasizing each word and encouraging me to picture it in my mind.

"It's raining. It's pouring. Charlie is...imploring
me to commune with nature.
She sits in her chair...sniffing the air,
hoping I learn the nomenclature."

His expectant grin had me putting a hand over my mouth to hold back my laughter.

"It...it was good," I giggled.

Axyl's chest puffed out. "It *was* good," he agreed proudly.

"I especially liked the part about nomenclature," I managed before another giggle erupted. "Big word bonus points.

"It's really no surprise. You're looking at Armadillo High's four time undefeated Scrabble champion. Bet you didn't know that about me." He sat back in his seat with a satisfied look.

I giggled again behind my hand. "Is that really a thing?"

He sat forward. "You don't believe me?" he asked, affronted.

I peered at him from behind the blanket, trying to figure him out.

"Ok," he finally conceded. "It's not a thing." He held up a finger. "But if it was, I would have been all over it."

"What did you do in high school, then, if it wasn't Scrabble? Chess?"

He brushed the comment aside with a sweep of his hand. "Nah. Sports."

"What sports?"

"Football. Basketball. Baseball."

My eyes widened. "All of them?"

"Yeah," he replied with a shrug.

"That explains…" my voice trailed off as my eyes ran the length of his blanket covered body and I realized what I had been about to say. I'd seen him in a swimming suit. I blushed and wanted to throw said blanket over my head, but didn't want to draw attention to my near verbal slip. By his sudden grin, he apparently noticed anyway. Thank heaven he was too kind- or too embarrassed, if his own slight blush was an indicator- to mention it.

"What do you do in high school? I mean besides the school newspaper?"

I shook my head.

"Not the school newspaper?" he asked, genuinely surprised. "I thought for sure with all the writing you do…Ok. An English club? A writing club?"

Again I shook my head.

"She does all the smart kids clubs," Brant said, joining us on the porch. "National Honor Society, AP everything, Academic Triathlon or Decathlon…"

I chuckled and Brant laughed at himself and shrugged.

Axyl studied me with wide eyes. "You really are a brainiac," he said. I appreciated that he didn't call me a nerd like Bailey always did.

I shrugged. School had always come easily to me. Now social situations…that was another thing entirely.

"No sports, though?" Axyl asked.

"I tried out for volleyball once."

Axyl nodded and gave me an encouraging smile.

"And for softball, but the only reason I made the team was for numbers."

"Oh, so they'd have enough to make up a team? Or like you'd go in if someone got injured?" Axly asked.

Brant snorted. "No. Like stats. She helped record stats. Numbers."

"I didn't know that was a position you had to try out for," Axyl said.

"Always the score keeper, never the scorer," I muttered.

Now he knew just how much of a nerd I really was. And I waited for him to laugh, but he never did.

"The stats guy…um girl is crucial to the game," he said instead.

Brant snorted again, but tried to cover it by commenting on how the storm had passed. I smacked his arm.

"Fine. Laugh," I told them. "But when your amazing touchdown, homerun, or three point game winning shot isn't on the news, or the college scout looks past you, you'll feel differently about the lowly stat girl."

"I'm feeling a new respect for the stat people," Axyl said, grinning at me. "And if they smell as good as you doing it..."

I rolled my eyes. "Thanks, Duncan," I said wryly, and stood, tossing my side of the blanket over his head before escaping into the cabin.

Brant's, "Duncan!? Whoa, man! She told you," and accompanying laughter followed me.

"That was low," came Axyl's muffled reply. But I heard him laugh too.

Idiots, I thought. But a smile tugged at my lips and my heart happily skipped right into the kitchen along with my cold feet.

Chapter 11

"You're starting college in the fall, Brant?" Iris asked, playing with a corner of her striped beach towel.

We were all sitting on towels and beach folding chairs the next afternoon on the little stretch of sand that paralleled the lake. Laney and Bailey were giggling and posing for selfies like models in an issue of Sports Illustrated and I had my nose in my notebook so I didn't have to watch them flaunt their beauty. It was as intriguing as it was embarrassing and I couldn't help but glance at Axyl out of the corner of one eye to see how often he looked their way while keeping close track of Duncan with my other eye so I could scoot farther away when he leaned over my shoulder to read my poems. I was running out of towel and patience.

"Yes." Brant said, breathing life into that one word. I frowned and studied my notebook in my lap, pretending not to listen to their conversation. Anyone could hear how happy he was about leaving.

Iris' hand moved from her towel to her hair, wrapping a lock around her finger and glancing shyly at Brant. "Where are you going?"

"You live in Colorado, right?" Brant asked with a teasing grin. Everyone laughed except for Iris who glanced at him coyly from beneath her lashes.

Duncan rested his chin on my shoulder and whispered, "He's not obvious or anything."

I slid over yet again while saying, "I think that was the point."

"Where are you going, Axyl?" Laney asked, puckering her lips and leaning into Bailey for another picture.

"Texas Tech," he replied, staring out over the lake.

Laney watched him with a pathetic pout on her face. Maybe she had been hoping for a similar reaction to the one Brant gave Iris.

"I can't wait to get away from here," Brant said. "It's the same people, the same places year after year. School can't start soon enough."

I tried to keep my eyes on my notebook as his words sliced into my heart, but I glanced up to see him watching me carefully. Had his words been meant for me specifically? Was I the one he couldn't wait to get away from? That thought hurt worse than his words.

"I know what you mean, man," Coleman replied easily. "Harvard law, here I come."

Wow! Impressive. And I could see in the raise of his brows that Brant was impressed as well.

"I'm not starting right back into school," Laney announced. "I need a break."

I snorted inside. Yes. Her life seemed very taxing as she lounged at the lake all day in the sun working on her tan.

Parker laughed. "She's not going to school because Mommy and Daddy are paying her to travel across Europe."

"Must be tough," Duncan snickered, grinning at me like we shared some sort of secret. Then, when Laney cried out, either at his tone or his words, he said, "You know we love you, Lane".

"I'm going to Europe after I graduate," Bailey told us.

"Good luck funding that," Brant said.

"You should come with me," Laney pouted prettily, reaching for Bailey's hand.

"What about you, Iris?" Brant asked. And I grinned at the way Iris colored under his attention.

But she kept her hands in her lap and studied them as she said, "I'm staying at the community college for a couple years."

I frowned. That seemed strange to me. All her friends were off to Ivy League colleges in the fall or *touring Europe* and she was going to the community college? I watched her from behind my notebook, noting how sadness filled her eyes and pulled her lips down. Was she sad about the community college or something else?

But she took a deep breath, squared her shoulders, and put on a smile. She really was pretty. And friendly. And I wished I was brave enough to pull her aside and ask if she was okay. Because she put up a good front, but I saw something painful just below the surface. Or maybe I'd imagined it. What did I know about people, really?

"I can't reach a spot on my back," Bailey announced, pushing a bottle of tanning oil at Axyl. "Will you get it for me, Ax?"

Axyl looked like a deer in headlights while Coleman and Brant smirked.

Duncan's chin found my shoulder again and he whispered, "I can help with your back if you need it."

I tried to ignore him, hoping he'd go away, but when he nudged my cheek with his nose, I rolled my eyes hard and stood, taking my towel with me. "Bailey and Laney could really use your help, Duncan."

"But I don't want to help Bailey or Laney," he argued, standing like he would follow me.

I held up a hand. "Don't Duncan," I said. "I want to be alone."

He gave me a look like someone kicked his dog and dropped back into the sand.

"Don't go," Iris called.

"I've had enough sun," I replied. "I'm going to go...somewhere." I raised a hand in a wave. "See you guys."

Isolation

Crowd
protection, shielding
Prison
inescapable, separation
Mind
seclusion, painful
Island
self-imposed, lonely
A pariah of my own making
                    -The Skinny Tomboy

I sat back in the tall grass and sighed in relief. I was far enough from the lake that I was by myself, but close enough to hear the occasional squeal of laughter from someone enjoying a summer afternoon on the water. Leaning on one hand, I stretched my legs out in front of me, crossing them at the ankles. The sun beat down on me, baking and calming at the same time. I glanced around my botanical oasis, satisfied that the tall grass hid me from the real world so I could escape. I lifted my pen to my mouth and reread my thoughts bleeding onto the page, waiting for my mind to rest as it always did after I got the words out.

But rest wouldn't come.

Was it bad to want to be alone? I wondered. Who said?

Until recently, I didn't question my choice. Wait. Was it a choice, or was I made this way?

I am who I am. I don't usually feel the need to apologize for that.

My isolation prevented awkward situations like the one I was just in where Duncan practically sat on my lap. I shivered now thinking of it. Too close. Too familiar. Too much…interaction.

I hadn't known how to handle it, so I'd left.

How do people know what to do? How do they retreat without appearing to?

Why couldn't I be more like Bailey? More like Brant? More like Iris?

I ran my palm across the grass.

"Ouch!" I yelped, yanking my hand back as the grass made a clean cut across my palm. I licked my hand, then shook it against the sting. Blood and salt mixed with my saliva and I rubbed my hand across my shorts.

I didn't know how to be anything other than me.

Now I felt trapped in my mind, knowing there was something more, but not knowing how to get it, to become it.

Voices sounded to my right and I froze. Grass swished near me and crunched under feet I couldn't see but could hear, getting closer before they eventually faded away.

Just as I'd hoped, the couple had passed by without even knowing I was there. I expected to feel satisfaction and reassurance. Instead, I felt unseen. Unknown.

That was the story of my life. Always on the periphery. Afraid. Uncertain. Alone.

What was the point of having a good idea if it was never shared?

If Brant never made anyone laugh, what was the use of being funny?

If Iris was never surrounded by a group, what was the use of being friendly?

If you never leave the nest, what's the use of growing up?

My next thought pierced and cut deeper than the grass. If I'm always on the outside, what's the use of being me?

But how can you change when you don't know how?

I ran up the cabin steps a while later and smacked into someone, almost falling back onto my butt. "Ooof! Geez, Brant." I scowled at him, still hurting from the look he gave me that let me know he couldn't wait to get away from me.

His brows rose at my tone. "What's the matter with you?" he asked.

"Nothing," I grouched.

"Whatever." He shrugged.

"How much longer did everyone stay at the lake?" I asked.

"Not much longer than you. Coleman had somewhere he needed to be." He leaned in and lowered his voice. "I think it was a date. So everyone else packed up and left too."

"You were just kidding with Iris, right? You aren't going to Colorado for school."

"No. But it would be fun. Especially because she's staying home." He waggled his brows for effect.

"You like her, huh?"

"She's okay. Better than Laney," he muttered.

I laughed.

"Don't laugh," Brant said. "Duncan was practically in your lap. I was ready to throw him in the lake."

"My protector," I teased. "Why do you think I left?"

And even though Brant's words really were sweet, that didn't mean I wasn't still mad at him. I looked at him through narrowed eyes.

"Just tell me, Charlie," he huffed. "I'm not going to wait around guessing."

"What's so bad about me that you can't wait to get out of here?" I asked, clearing my throat to keep the tears at bay.

"What are you talking about?" he asked.

"You told everyone that you can't wait to get out of here for school and you looked at me specifically."

"I was watching you to see how you would take what I had to say, not because I was hinting that you're the reason I'm leaving."

"You promise?" I sniffed.

"Of course I promise. Stop being ridiculous. You know I'll miss you more than anyone." He reached out and mussed my hair in that obnoxious way brothers do.

"Are you sure you have to go?" I whispered, smoothing my hair that he'd just pawed through. My ability to ignore his actions only extends so far.

"I'm leaving, Charlie," he stated. "I know you hate it, but I'm leaving."

I stared at my feet and nodded silently. I hated the tears that welled in my eyes, but there was no way to hold them back this time.

"But that doesn't mean," he began, shoving me gently on the shoulder, "that we won't ever see each other again. I'll be home some weekends and for the entire summer next year."

"I guess," I admitted with a sniff, though I still hated it.

"And Thanksgiving and Christmas."

I nodded, feeling somewhat appeased. Though I knew those times wouldn't make up for the day to day chats.

"After I get back from my orphanage trip in Mexico-" I began.

"You're not going to Mexico, Charlie," Brant interrupted with a hard laugh.

I paused, my eyebrows pulling together in confusion. Did he know something I didn't? "Not going? What?"

He snorted. "The only places you go are school and here." He gestured to the cabin and lake with a swing of his arm. "You can't even pick a different spot for a vacation. How are you going to go to another country by yourself for six weeks?" He searched my face, a frown tugging down his usually smiling lips. "Not happening," he concluded with a sad shake of his head.

I stared open mouthed at him as the truth of his words resonated in my heart. Six weeks by myself in a foreign country with people I didn't know.

No Mom.

No Dad.

No Brant.

Not even Bailey.

My gut churned and my breathing came quickly.

Who else thought my humanitarian trip was just a big joke?

Brant was right. I couldn't even take a different route home from school on a whim. I couldn't talk to anyone at school unless assigned to by a teacher. I couldn't get behind the wheel of a car. And I couldn't even be angry with him because what he said was true.

I knew I drove him crazy sometimes with my inability to adventure, but it wasn't legit crazy. He indulged me and smiled, picked up the conversation and steered the attention away from me before situations became awkward. Sheltered me like a doting big brother should. But he'd never been mean or made me feel stupid about it.

If I wanted brutal honesty...that was Bailey's department.

If anyone understood me, it was Brant. He'd always helped me through, teasing me out of myself.

Had Brant been lying to me all this time?

I turned away from him and slowly made my way down the stairs to the gravel road. But where was I going to go? I looked around, seeing everything, but nothing at the same time. I staggered down the road with no destination in mind. It didn't matter where I went anyway.

Brant was right. I was wrong. I couldn't change.

I had been fooling myself.

The Fool

She flits around from person to person, all giggly and innocent touches.

Silly.

He laughs loudly at the crowd so everyone thinks he understands, clueless yet charismatic.

Half-wit.

He bulldozes through unwanted conversation with an inviting look in his eye, puffed up and awkward.

Buffoon.

She sees it all, yet sees nothing.

In a room full of people pretending to be something they are not,
The only fool is me.

-The Skinny Tomboy

Chapter 12

I ended up back down at the lake. Big surprise there. I stared at the water, unseeing, and chewed on the end of my pen. Even though I felt humiliated by the words I had to write, I also felt better now that they were on paper. I could close the book and put the emotions away from me. They were no longer rolling around in my mind, mocking me. I could deal with them now and maybe not be such an idiot in the future.

I dragged my eyes from the lake when a faint cry of frustration sounded off to my left somewhere. A boy about six or seven was standing in the water just off the bank. He smacked a hand down, making a small, flat splash, and growled. Tucking my pen in my notebook, I set it aside and watched the boy. He appeared to be trying to find something. But from the noises of defeat coming from him, I deduced he wasn't succeeding.

I looked around for a possible parent or sibling before standing and walking up the dock and along the edge of the lake.

"What ya doing?" I asked, bending over and peering into the semi-stagnant water.

The boy did a double take when I spoke to him and then sighed. "See that?" he asked, pointing a short finger at a clump of algae waving lazily in the water in front of him. "There's a frog in there."

I went down to my haunches and leaned over. Sure enough. There, camouflaged among the greens and browns of nature, was a frog. Its long legs gave a push and it skirted through the boy's hands and disappeared.

"See?!" the boy cried, disappointed. "It's too fast."

I looked around us and frowned, thinking. "You have a cup or something?" I asked.

His eyes lit up and he held up a finger. "I'll be right back," he cried, sloshing through the shallow water and clambering up onto the bank. He took off at a run, calling, "Mom! I need a cup!"

I smiled and parted the tall grass, carefully making my way into the water. Striders and mayflies floated on the surface amidst rising bubbles and white foam. Mud suctioned my flip flops to the lake bed and slid between my toes. I wiggled them back and forth, feeling the grittiness.

I stood motionless and searched for the frog in the place the boy had shown me. It wasn't long before I spotted the expert hider. Keeping one eye on it, I looked to the base of the tree where a mother searched through camping gear for a cup.

Only a moment passed before the boy turned to me, holding a cup high in the air. I grinned and waved him over.

"I found him," I whispered, holding out my hand for the cup when the boy stood on the bank in front of me.

He craned his neck to see where I pointed and an excited grin filled his face. "I see him! I see him!" he exclaimed. I chuckled silently knowing that was about as quiet as an enthusiastic frog catcher could be under the circumstances.

I held the cup in one hand and raised the other in the air before creeping forward slowly. "You need to use both hands," I explained softly. "One to hold the cup, and the other to put over the top to keep him in when I catch him."

He solemnly nodded his understanding. I knew he took our work very seriously. I crept closer to the frog, my hands poised and ready. Out of the corner of my eye, I saw the boy lean so far over the bank in anticipation that I worried he'd fall in. But I had to trust he would be okay because now was the time.

Acting quickly, I lunged forward, scooping the frog into the cup and slapping my hand down on the top.

"Did ya get him?" the boy yelled. "Did ya get him?"

I grinned at him, triumphantly holding the cup up for his inspection.

The boy threw his fist in the air and cheered, "You got him! Let's go show my mom."

I trudged through the water, easing each foot out of the mud repeatedly until I made it to the bank. I wiggled my feet in the water to get the mud off and followed the boy to the tree where his mother sat, wide eyed.

"She caught him, Mom," the boy said. "Wanna see?"

"Here," I said, pushing the cup to the boy. "You show her." I handed him the cup, keeping my hand over the top. "Slide your hand under mine. Keep it down tight."

The cup shifted in the transfer and the frog jumped in his prison, touching the palm of the boy's hand. He started and threw the cup to the ground.

"Oh, no!" he cried, scrambling after the frog. But the amphibian was on a mission. We watched it hop back to the water and jump in, getting farther and farther away from us with long, sure strokes. "Darn!" he muttered.

"Don't worry," I said. "We can catch another one." I motioned for him to follow me.

He picked up the cup and raced past me. "We'll get another one, Mom!" he hollered over his shoulder.

I smiled at his optimism.

"Thank you," his mother called with a smile.

I returned her smile with one of my own and followed the boy back into the water. We waded closer to the dock this time, hoping that was a location more frogs frequented. We were rewarded when we saw three croakers floating motionless in the water.

The sandy-haired boy, eyes alight, moved stealthily forward. I stood back and watched. Suddenly, he sprang forward, catching a cup full of lake water and a frog in one motion. I laughed at his look of shock.

"Other hand! Other hand!" I reminded him.

He slammed his hand down onto the top of the cup just as three skinny, padded fingers wrapped around the rim.

"Whoa," the little hunter breathed. "That was close."

"It sure was," I chuckled. "But you got him. Good job."

"Thanks," he said proudly before peeking between his fingers to study his catch. "He's a pretty good looking frog."

I nodded, amused. This kid didn't have a care in the world. I wondered as I watched him when the simple things had become more complicated for me. When had I begun noticing and being bogged down by cares?

"You want another turn?" he asked, interrupting my stray thoughts and holding the cup out to me. I only had a moment to wonder where the frog had gone when he pulled the cup back as an idea hit him. "Wait a sec. I'll go get another cup, then we won't have to wait for each other." He headed swiftly for the bank, clearly proud of his genius plan.

I smiled. I hadn't minded waiting. But I answered, "Good idea."

He was back in under a minute with a second cup. "My mom says I can only stay for a little while longer cause I'm starting to turn pink, so it's a good thing I got my own cup." He held it up. "That way we can catch more."

"What will you do with them when you catch them?" I asked, distracted. I'd just seen one right next to the dock, and I was moving toward it, poised and ready, and only partially listening to my new friend's answer. It was just me in the dock's shadow, my cup, and the four-legged, green amphibians.

"Nice day for a swim," a male voice said in my ear. Startled, I yelped and whipped around, upsetting my balance. I windmilled my arms and tried to adjust my feet, but the thick mud held my flip flops captive. I tugged and my feet pulled loose, minus the flip flops, and slipped across the slick mud. I went down, cup and all.

I surfaced to see Brant and Axyl lying on their stomachs on the dock, chins resting on their arms, with huge cheesy grins plastered to their handsome faces.

"What'cha doin'?" Brant asked innocently.

I glared at them, feeling around the bottom for my flip flops. I finally located them and slid my feet into them, tugging them up to free them. I pushed hair out of my face and wiped the remaining water from my eyes.

"We're catching frogs," my young accomplice explained, handing my cup to me. His voice held an unspoken reprimand.

"And you just made us miss one," I chided.

Axyl's brows rose. "You're catching frogs?" he asked, a bit of disgust tinting his words.

I shrugged. "Yeah. So?" I stared at him, challenging him to tell me that's not something girls should do.

But all he said was, "Cool."

"You wanna try it?" the boy asked, squinting up at the two men.

Panic flitted across Axyl's face before he could school his features. *Hm. He's afraid of something,* I thought. *Not the water. He'd been kayaking with us. Frogs?* It was funny, but I wouldn't laugh. And I wouldn't call him on it.

But it was Brant who answered for both of them. "Nah," he said. "It's more fun watching Charlie drown herself."

"We've already caught two," the boy boasted. "Watch and learn."

Then I did laugh. I liked this kid.

So Axyl and Brant gave us their rapt attention as we silently stalked our next victims. They spent more time laughing at my frantic movements and splashing than anything else. And as the fearless hunter's mother called to him, I got an idea.

I turned my back to Brant and Axyl and whispered, "I'm going to play a trick on those boys." My young friend's eyes got big and he peeked around me to grin at them. "No! Don't look or else they'll know we're doing something."

He sucked his cheeks in to smother his smile and nodded eagerly.

I scooped up a cup of water and clamped my hand down over the opening. "Got one!" I exclaimed loudly, sharing a mischievous smile with the boy.

"No you didn't," Brant objected.

"Yes she did," the sunburned boy said, attempting to keep a grin off his freckled face.

"Yeah. Wanna see?" I walked slowly over to them, holding the cup with both hands the way I'd shown the boy. When they both leaned in, I removed my hand from the top of the cup. Instead of a frog, dirty lake water splashed into their faces. They sputtered and blinked, and the boy laughed uproariously. He held his fist up and gave me knuckles just as his mother's voice reached us for the second time.

His smile turned down. "Gotta go," he said. "Here's your cup. Thanks for catching frogs with me."

I watched as he ran to his mother, took her outstretched hand, and talked a million miles a minute, filling her in, I guessed, on all our adventures. Before the distance between us got too big, he paused and looked back. Spotting me on the dock, he waved.

What a cute kid.

"You got water up my nose," Brant complained as we walked back to the cabin.

"That's nothing," I said, glancing at Axyl out of the corner of my eye. Maybe I would call him on it after all. "Wait until you see what I brought with me." I made a big deal of carefully digging around inside my towel and abruptly tossed my empty cup at Axyl.

He jerked back with a very unmasculine shriek. "Not the frog!" I pointed at him, laughing. "You were scared."

Axyl scowled at me as he picked up the cup.

Brant was bent over at the waist in laughter. "She got you, man!" he managed. "I'm not sure what's gotten into her, but she got you."

I tried but failed to hold back my smug grin until Axyl hooked an arm around my neck and dragged me along behind him. Then I laughed outright.

"You and me," he said, propelling me forward. "Right now. Uno competition."

"So I can embarrass you again?" I asked with a laugh, still stumbling along beside him.

"Last one to the cabin deals," he said, suddenly removing his arm from my neck and sprinting ahead.

"Loser eats burned marshmallows at the campfire tonight," I hollered after him.

"That won't be a problem for you," he returned. "I know how much you love them."

I snorted, turning around to wave at Brant to pick up the pace as I broke into a jog.

"I'm staying out of this," Brant called. "Go kick his designer butt. Make me proud."

Chapter 13

The next day, I grabbed the knotted end of the rope from the split in the log where a previous user had wedged it for the next person- me- and turned to hike a ways up the side of the mountain.

I was feeling pretty invincible after my Uno sweep the night before. Axly ate so many burned marshmallows, I didn't understand how he wasn't sick. Of course, it turned into an eating contest between Brant, Axle, Coleman, and Duncan. I was gagging just watching them. Iris laughed so hard watching me gag while watching them that I'm sure the reason she excused herself in the middle of the fun was to sprint to the bathroom before she peed herself.

Now I stood on the side of the mountain, rope in hand, and inhaled deeply. I'd show Brant that I was brave. I could do scary things. And without anyone holding my hand.

When I turned back toward the water, the ground spun beneath my feet. Whoa! It was really high. I slid down the mountain a foot before digging in my heels to keep me from going over before I was ready and drew in another deep breath. Others made it look so easy. I closed my eyes to center myself. This was as difficult as I'd anticipated, which is why I'd never done it.

But I had to do it. Today. Now.

Taking the rope in both hands, one right above the other, I prepared to swing out into the lake.

"Hey!"

A male voice startled me and I glanced up, losing my footing and sliding again. I kept a hold of the rope and dragged my feet, kicking up rocks and dust, but slowing myself enough to keep me from going over the edge out of control and belly flopping on the lake.

Josh stepped up beside me and glanced over the edge. "That was close," he commented.

You think? Instead of saying anything, though, I adjusted my grip on the rope and turned and hiked back up the mountain to try again.

"Have you ever done this before?" he asked my back.

"No."

"Are you scared?"

I rolled my eyes, wishing he'd leave. While I didn't care about his opinion, I didn't want my failure to be common knowledge if this ended badly. That's why I hadn't told Brant where I was going.

"Did you come up here to swing too?" I asked, offering him the rope. "Because you can go first. I'll wait till you're finished."

He took a few steps off the trail and folded his arms across his chest. "That's okay. I can wait." He smiled at me, letting me know he'd enjoy every minute of watching me career off the side of the mountain into the water below.

I dropped the rope and wiped my hands on my shorts.

"That's okay," I said, walking down the trail and skirting around him. "I changed my mind."

"But you haven't even gone yet."

"There's always tomorrow."

"Hey. Come here," he called after me. "I don't bite."

"No thanks," I answered, speeding up a bit.

I heard the rapid crunch of gravel as he jogged to catch up and sighed.

I spun on him. "What do you want?" I asked, folding my arms across my chest and cocking a hip.

"You don't need to get all...like that," he said, waving a hand at my 'back off' stance.

"What do you want, Josh?"

He grinned when I said his name like he got a certain sense of satisfaction out of it.

"I wanted to ask you to go into the city with me for dinner tonight."

I took a step back, shaking my head. He'd followed me to ask me out? "Uh, no thanks."

"Why not?"

"I don't know you," I said.

"Go out with me, and you will," he replied like it was that simple.

I scoffed. "I'm not eighteen," I informed him.

"I don't care...if you don't." He reached behind him and pulled something out of the waistband of his shorts. "I got you this."

I swallowed hard and stared at the notebook he held out to me like it was a diamond back rattler.

"That's nice of you," I managed, "but I can't take it."

"Yes you can." He grabbed my hand and shoved the book into it, but I pulled my hand away like the snake had struck, and the book dropped to the dirt trail.

He frowned and bent to pick it up. "Now look what you did."

"I'm sorry," I said, honestly. "I hope I didn't ruin it."

He turned it over slowly in his hands, inspecting it. "You have to take it now. It would be rude not to."

"I'm not trying to be rude," I insisted. "I just can't take that from you."

"Why don't you like me?" he asked. "Are you afraid of me?

I opened my mouth to answer, but didn't know what to say. I wasn't afraid of him exactly, but I also didn't get warm fuzzies when he was around.

"Just like with the rope swing," he said, taking a step closer to me, "you have to try me out before you can have an opinion." He raised his eyebrows in a challenge and grinned suggestively. "I promise you'll like it."

Yuck! And...No. Stinking. Way.

"Hey, Charlie! You up here?" Brant called. I could hear footsteps on rocks then and tree branches brushing against something. I wanted to cry, I was so relieved to hear his voice.

Josh stepped back, shoving the book wherever he took it from and gave me one more lingering look before heading down the mountain.

Brant and Axyl passed Josh on their way up. I watched on wobbly knees as they approached, so I saw the moment when Brant thought about taking Josh out with his shoulder as they walked past, but after a split second of indecision, his eyes found mine and he forgot about Josh.

"What ya doing up here?" he asked.

"I was going to do the rope swing," I replied as casually as I could.

Brant frowned. "With that loser?" he asked, nodding his head in the direction they'd come.

"What do you think, Brant?" I replied, disgusted that he thought so little of me.

"Well, before now I wouldn't have thought you'd come up here at all." He watched me through narrowed eyes. "What are you doing, Charlie?"

"I think the better question, Brant, is is she okay?" Axyl asked, eyeing me closely.

I nodded and looked at the ground. Josh hadn't done anything except touch my hand, so why did I feel violated?

"You should probably stay away from him," Axyl suggested.

"I didn't seek him out," I argued. "He followed me."

"Then you shouldn't go anywhere alone," Brant said, frowning. "I don't know what it is about you..." he shook his head.

"What what is about me?" I asked, my voice rising. "This wasn't my fault."

"I never said it was," Brant replied.

"Well, you're acting like it was."

"What did he want anyway?" Brant asked. I noticed Axyl didn't look any less interested in my answer.

"He asked me out. Wanted to give me something." I shrugged like it was more harmless than it had felt at the time.

"What?" Brant demanded.

"It wasn't anything much," I said, embarrassed by the notebook Josh had placed in my hand because it was an item that meant a lot to me and somehow he'd figured that out.

"Then why won't you tell us?"

"Because it wasn't important," I grouched. "Forget about it." I lowered my voice. "Please."

Brant sighed and looked back at the trail that Josh had disappeared down. He looked back at me, studying my face.

"So are you ever going to be a real woman and conquer the rope swing?" Brant asked, grinning. I felt my mouth turn up into a matching grin, grateful that he'd dropped it. The teasing was a good sign. "It feels like this is your year."

I was feeling significantly less brave than I'd felt ten minutes ago. I waved a dismissive hand at the rope. "I'll leave that to you," I said.

"I think she just called you a girl, Brant." Axyl chuckled.

"No," I disagreed, my grin broadening. "I called both of you girls."

Brant grunted a laugh. "I know you're scared, Charlie. Let us help you."

I shook my head and turned to get the rope before he could. Past experience had shown me that his help was less than helpful.

"I've got it. But thanks."

Before I knew what was happening, Brant scrambled past me, grabbed the rope, and charged me.

I only had time to cry out in surprise before we were flying over the water. I clung to Brant's neck with my arms and my legs wrapped his waist like a vice.

"Stupid, Brant!" I screamed. "Stupid, stupid!"

He just laughed as we swung back over land, spinning out of control. "We'll be over the water in two seconds. That's when I'm letting go."

I clung tighter. We were going to die!

"You're pulling my shorts off," Brant complained.

"That's going to be the least of your worries if we live," I ground out.

"Ready?"

"No! No! I changed my mind. I don't want to do this."

"Tooo laate!" Brant hollered as he let go and we free fell.

The entire thing- from Brant grabbing me to hitting the water- only took fifteen seconds, max, but I lived a lifetime in those harrowing seconds.

The shock of the cool water yanked my breath from my lungs. I kicked as soon as I submerged. When I broke the surface, I sucked in air, treading water, and looked around to find Brant.

"Cannonball!" Axyl shouted, flying out over the water. I watched through strands of dripping hair as he made it look effortless. He let go of the rope and flipped one time in the air before dropping straight into the water, pointing his toes and barely making a splash. Show off!

He came up with a grin of pure delight on his handsome face. We swam toward Brant, reaching him at the same time.

"How was it?" Axyl wanted to know.

"I should thank Brant, but I won't." I swiped at Brant's head, attempting to push him under. He resisted with a hand around my wrist. I went behind him and pushed down on both his shoulders with my whole weight, raising myself out of the water.

"You're so tough, Charlie," Brant said, laughing at my attempt to push him under. "You should climb back up and do it again."

I scowled at him as I swam away. I'd show him. I would climb back up and I would do it by myself.

And I did.

•••••

Half an hour later, the three of us spread out on a boulder near the edge of a diving cliff in the sun.

"Hey, Charlie," Brant said, poking my side.

I swatted at him. "What?" I asked groggily, turning over onto my back and resting an arm across my eyes to block out the sun. "I was almost asleep."

"Good job today," he said quietly. "I'm sorry for what I said the other day about you not making it on that humanitarian trip. You're different this summer. I almost think you won't die without us for the two months you'll be gone."

I turned my head enough to peer at him from one eye. "Gee, thanks."

Brant chuckled. "What's with all the sarcasm lately?"

"I don't know," I said around a yawn. "Maybe I've just finally had enough of your crap and I'm fighting back the only way I know how."

"I like it," he replied.

"Can I ask you something?" I asked, peeking at Axyl on Brant's other side. He was sleeping like a cat in the sun.

"Sure."

"How do you do it?"

"How do I do what?" he asked, looking at me.

"How do you talk to people like it's no big deal? How are you so comfortable around everyone? I hate that I'm scared. That I don't know what to say or how to act. I'm tired of being on the outside." My voice cracked and I swallowed, hoping to clear the emotion.

Brant sat up, propping up a knee and resting his arm on it, and faced me. "I honestly don't know," he said. "I know that doesn't help, and I'm sorry. It's not something I have to think about. I just do it."

"I can't talk to anyone without my hands sweating. I'm afraid I'll say something stupid." I gestured to him and Axyl's still form. "You guys already laugh at me."

"You and Iris get along," he pointed out.

"That's because she's like you. She could get a rock to talk to her. She's not afraid and she's super nice."

Brant smiled.

"Even Bailey can talk to anyone. I'm so socially awkward, though."

"I've seen you talk to Duncan," Brant said, holding up a hand when I objected that Duncan didn't count. "It doesn't matter if you like him or not," Brant told me. "You still talk to him. And Axyl. You've talked to him a ton. I've actually been surprised." He glanced over his shoulder to check on Axyl and lowered his voice. "That's why I teased you about liking him. Because you talked to him like I've never seen you do with anyone besides me and Mom before."

I hated that my face turned red. But what he said was true. Once I decided to give Axyl a chance, I was able to talk to him without worrying that I'd say something stupid. Maybe it was because he didn't give me a choice. He forced his way into my space in a non-threatening, though often annoying, way. I didn't even realize he was doing it, and before I knew it, we'd been talking for twenty minutes or more.

"You don't give yourself enough credit," Brant said. "If you just speak up and say something…don't give yourself time to think about it because you psych yourself out. Just choose one person a day and say hi. Nothing else. Just hello. The next day, choose someone else. When that doesn't feel hard anymore, add a compliment: Your brother's sick. Your sister's a drama queen. That kind of thing."

I laughed. "I'd be giving the compliments, lame-o, not taking them."

Brant grinned. "So you admit that your brother's all that."

I shook my head and picked up a pebble by my side and threw it at him. "No way."

"You don't have to give a speech. Just start small. You'll be carrying on a conversation before you know it. And you won't even have puked from nerves."

"I've never done that," I scoffed.

"There's a first time for everything," Brant replied.

"Thanks, Brant," I said softly, blinking the sudden emotion away.

"You can come to me anytime for advice," he said, puffing up. "I know everything."

I rolled my eyes.

"I've been thinking..." He leaned closer and lowered his voice again. "If I take Axyl's arms and you take his legs, we could throw him over the cliff. He wouldn't even know what hit him."

"I heard that," Axyl muttered, making me jump.

"It was just a thought," Brant said. "You were sleeping so peacefully."

"I wasn't asleep," Axyl told him. "I heard everything you guys said. It was interesting up until you plotted to take my life."

Brant chuckled.

"You know how people say when you dream about falling off a cliff if you hit the ground in real life, you'd die...?" I asked, pondering. "If Axyl had really been asleep just now and we threw him off the cliff, would he have died when he hit the water?"

Brant barked a laugh. "Don't worry about me, Axyl," he laughed. "It's Charlie you really need to watch out for."

"No doubt," Axyl said, rolling to his stomach and pushing up with his arms to hop to his feet. "That's twisted. And you know what I have to say about that?" he asked, walking toward me.

My eyes popped open at his tone and I regarded him warily. "I don't care," I said quickly.

"You'll care in about two seconds," he said, hovering over me, mischief in his eyes.

I held up a hand as I struggled to sit up. "You leave me alone." But Brant had hopped to his feet as well and was advancing. I didn't like the look in his eyes. I held up my other hand. "Don't touch me, Brant."

"But you're so good at jumping into the water now."

My eyes grew big as I got the first hint of what he was threatening. I scurried to my feet and backed up.

"The swing is different," I said, panicked.

"Not that much different," Axyl replied. "On three, Brant."

But they didn't even give me till two before both of them rushed me, each grabbing an arm, and leaped into the air with me.

I screamed and scrabbled in the air, not finding anything to cling to as I fell thirty feet to the water below.

So much for the caring older brother of a minute ago.

"I hate you!" I yelled. "I hate you both."

Chapter 14

Genetics
I don't claim you as part of me
Not usually nor on purpose
Even though I have no choice
But there is that moment- rare and shocking- when I take you
into my heart and close the door as a response to you opening
yours.
We won't speak of it again.
Painful and confining
But I will claim you- if only for that moment- as part of me.
Not usually. But this one time.
Even though I have no choice
                    -The Skinny Tomboy

"What ya writing about today?" Axyl asked, dropping down next to me on the dock like he had so many times in the past two weeks.

I put my pen in my book and set it beside me, smiling up at him. "Stuff," I said.

"That's eloquent." He sent me an appraising look. "You know, I think you've been lying to me for weeks now."

My brows pulled together. "What are you talking about?" I asked.

"That notebook...it's not a bunch of poems. It's probably full of words like blah-blah-blah."

I sucked in an offended breath.

"Are you ever going to let me read one?" he asked.

I shook my head. My answer was definitely no after what he'd just said.

"Come on. We're running out of time," he reminded me.

Three days to be exact. The time had passed so quickly. I felt like I didn't know anything about him, but only because I knew there was so much more to learn. I had only scratched the surface and this was the only opportunity I'd ever have.

Something like panic welled in my chest.

I understood a little better now why he and Brant wanted to avoid attachments before leaving for school. When one of you walked away, there was a nothingness that filled the space they used to occupy. It played tricks with your mind to the point that you wondered if they'd ever really been there to begin with. Or maybe you just imagined their presence in your life.

"If it's really poetry, you should let me look. You know, so I believe you."

I pressed my lips together. What would it hurt really? Like I'd just said, I wouldn't ever see him again.

I picked up my notebook and thumbed through the pages, finally deciding on one.

> *You*
> *A mystery I don't want to solve*
> *A fear I don't want to face*
> *A chance I don't want to take*
> *A life I won't live*
> *Me*
> *-The Skinny Tomboy*

I handed him the book. He paused before taking it from me, giving me the chance to change my mind. I didn't.

I watched him as he read, hoping to see something in his expression that would tell me what he thought, what he felt. What if he didn't feel anything? Would that be better or worse than him feeling something?

His lips moved with the words and he nodded when he got to the end.

"Do you want me to comment?" he asked, closing the book and handing it back to me.

I opened my mouth to speak, but no words came out. I cleared my throat and tried again.

"Only if you want to," I told him. "Don't say something just to talk. It would mean more to me that you stay silent rather than saying something you don't feel."

Again he nodded.

I waited, wondering if he would say anything now or make up an excuse to walk away.

He swallowed and said, "I know it's none of my business, and you didn't know I was listening in yesterday on the rocks, so I hope it's okay to say. I have a friend back home who has some anxiety. He's mentioned how his hands sweat. How he doesn't know what to say. He panics. He can't breathe.

"His parent's take him to a therapist who gives him exercises that access the part of the brain that produces anxiety. He also has breathing techniques that help when he's in an uncomfortable situation. Maybe you could ask your parents to help you find someone to talk to. They can teach you stuff, give you tools to help." He shrugged, not meeting my eyes. "It's just a thought."

"Thank you, Axyl," I said, honestly touched by his concern. "I appreciate it."

"Well," he said, finally meeting my eyes. "I'm not like Brant. I don't know everything." I snorted and he grinned. "But everyone has issues with something. It's nothing to be ashamed of. And if there are people out there who can help, I say use all the resources you have."

"I was buying all your psycho-mumbo-jumbo up until you said everyone has issues," I told him. "You don't. Brant doesn't."

He leaned closer, his eyes intent. "Just because we don't tell you what they are doesn't mean they don't exist." He sat back, putting some distance between us. "Besides, I think you're pretty cool the way you are."

I stared at him, wondering if he'd really just said that. "Thanks," I whispered. "I guess you're okay too."

He chuckled and wrapped an arm around me in a side hug.

"This will now go down as the greatest summer of my life," he said. "Charlie admitted she likes me." I opened my mouth to object, so he hurried to clarify. "Did I say *likes* me? Sorry. I meant she *tolerates* me."

"That's better," I said with a small laugh, though I was dying inside.

"You're really leaving, huh?" I asked, suddenly wishing he was staying for the rest of the summer.

"Yeah. I probably better leave when my parents do. I have thought about walking home, but…"

"You're always ready for an adventure," I teased.

"Some adventures have to wait," he said, his voice going soft.

Were we talking about the same thing anymore? Suddenly I wasn't sure.

"I wanted to tell you thank you for including me the past two weeks," he said. "I know it's not easy for you, so it means more to me that you let me invade your safe place."

"I guess I can admit that it wasn't as bad as I thought it would be." I held up a finger and said, "And one day, you'll be sitting at work or stuck in traffic, or trying to stay awake through some class, and you'll wish you were back here."

"I'll wish I was back here, huh?" he asked, his voice low. "In this exact spot? Is that a promise?"

I cleared my throat of the nervousness clawing its way to the surface. "Well, maybe not in this *exact* spot," I managed. "But yes. You'll wish this back."

He studied me for a time, unblinking, before focusing on something out in front of us. And then I felt dumb. When had my life become so complex and confusing? Oh, right. The minute I let emotion for Axyl rule me. That's why I kept things intellectual. It was less ambiguous.

He reached over and took my hand in his. "Thank you for trusting me with your poem." He gave my hand a squeeze then rose to his feet and offered me a smile before he turned and walked up the dock.

Chapter 15

"Sunrise hike in the morning," Dad called through the cabin later that night as we all settled into our beds.

"I hate that hike," Bailey grumbled.

"Isn't it about a month early for that hike, Dad?" I heard Brant ask.

Brant's question was the same one I had. For as far back as I could remember, Dad insisted on a three mile round trip family hike to watch the sun rise every summer the morning before we left to go back home. It wasn't strenuous, but there was always a life lesson he tried to incorporate that sounded a bit like preaching. It always felt too early in the morning to find life applications.

"I decided I want the Stewarts to experience it with us this year. We'll leave at four thirty. And yes, everyone has to go."

We'd each tried backing out over the years, but we decided to go along with it after he dragged Brant's mattress through the cabin, out the door and down the stairs the summer Brant was fourteen. Brant was still on the mattress. In his underwear. After that, we realized Dad meant business and it was just easier to go on the hike. The sunrises were spectacular and worth the loss of sleep.

The next morning, Bailey and I stumbled down the stairs in the dark, pulling hoodies over our heads. We met up with Brant and Axyl in the kitchen.

"I say we stage a mutiny," Brant grumbled, still wiping the sleep from his eyes. "He can't take us all on together."

Axyl ran a hand through his bed head, attempting to tame the most stubborn parts. It didn't work. And it was adorable.

"Grab a granola bar or two," Dad instructed, coming into the kitchen. "Make sure you have water." He was way too happy for this time of day.

We all took turns looking at each other questioningly as Dad opened the fridge and took out a watermelon. Even Mom and Kristin shared a look of uncertainty.

"Is that breakfast?" Brant asked, suddenly awake at the thought of food.

"Not yet."

"What does that mean?" Bailey asked around a yawn.

"You'll see," Dad replied with a smile I didn't trust.

"Matt," Dad said, "I wondered if you would carry this watermelon for us on the hike."

"Sure," Matt said, taking it from Dad.

"You'd better let me carry that, Dad," Axyl said. "I don't want you to hurt yourself."

Brant gave Axyl knuckles and they both laughed. They were a lot alike. Too much, maybe. Living with Brant's teasing all my life and now seeing how Axyl loved to laugh and tease, I realized that maybe I'd been too hard on him when they'd first arrived. Like Brant, Axyl's teasing wasn't meant to be mean. He didn't single anyone out and tease repeatedly. He didn't bully. He just liked to have fun and that was one of the ways he did it.

"If we're going to make it by sunrise, we'd better get going," Dad said.

We shoved granola bars and water bottles into cinch sacks and set out on the hike with Dad in the lead. Matt and the watermelon brought up the rear with the rest of us somewhere in between.

Fifteen minutes in, Dad told Matt to pass the watermelon to someone else. Of course he gave it to Axyl with some good-natured teasing about staying right behind him in case it got too heavy.

I carried the watermelon for the last leg of our journey. We had to pick up our speed at the end to make the sunrise. My arms felt stretched and wobbly. My breath puffed from me with the exertion of the added weight.

But then..there it was. The sun rose out of the ground in all its glory, turning the sky pink and apricot as we crested the last hill. I stopped, speechless, and nearly dropped the watermelon. The scene was breathtaking.

"Is there a certain way we appreciate this?" Axyl asked, leaning down to whisper in my ear as if he felt the reverence of the scene also.

"Uh…no," I stuttered.

"Just making sure it isn't like a rainstorm. I want to get the full effect."

"To get the full effect, you have to stand with your mouth hanging partially open and your eyes wide," I instructed.

"Like this?" he asked, copying me. Only his eyes were crossed.

I laughed softly. "Exactly like that."

"Is something supposed to happen?" he asked after a time.

"You don't feel any different?" I asked.

"I feel like an idiot," he grumbled.

"Then you're doing it right."

He gave me a small shove and I laughed.

"I'm going to go sit on the ridge," I told him. "You can come if you want."

He followed me and we sat down in silence, side by side, our legs dangling over the edge.

I rummaged in my pack for my notebook, realizing I'd forgotten it. What?

"You better write this down," Axyl said, bumping me with his shoulder, though he stared straight ahead.

"Would you believe I left it at the cabin?" I asked, shocked.

Now Axyl turned to me. "No. I don't believe you."

I handed my pack over. "See for yourself."

He made a show of searching the bag, putting as much of himself in as he could fit.

"I'm glad we made it to see the sunrise, because I think it's our last," he said gravely, removing his head from the bag. "The world has to be coming to an end."

I snatched the bag back from him. "Funny. I'll compose in my head and write it down later."

I was just finishing the first line in my head when Dad called us to gather around him. He removed a knife from a sheath on his belt. We all watched as he sliced into the watermelon. Juice bled from the cut and darkened the soil beneath it. The aroma that filled the small space around us made my mouth water.

"Who wants the first slice?" Dad asked, holding out a triangular wedge.

"I do," Brant said, taking it from Dad. He didn't waste any time or manners tearing into the juicy sweet fruit. He made a slurping noise, but the juice ran down his arm anyway. "Mmmm."

Axyl took the next piece, followed by Matt.

Pretty soon, all of us were happily munching on a refreshing slice of summer.

"Hey Charlie," Brant called, "Catch."

I turned in time to feel a watermelon seed flick my cheek and fall to the ground beside me.

"Did you just spit a seed at me?" I demanded, swiping at my cheek.

Brant nodded, laughing. "And I'm going to do it again."

I put up a hand to shield my face from any more seeds.

"Brant," Mom's voice was a warning. But Brant didn't listen. Another seed flew at me and landed on the sleeve of my t-shirt.

"At least spit for distance," Mom suggested, "instead of spitting at each other."

Brant hopped up, taking another slice of watermelon with him and walked a ways off. "Charlie," he called, "you stay by the trail and Axyl and I will spit from the grass here. Tell us which one hits closest to the trail."

I rolled my eyes, but stood, walking to my designated spot and watched Brant spit seeds from his mouth in rapid succession like a machine gun. None of the seeds hit their mark.

"You're too far away," I told him. "Take a couple steps in."

Axyl, Brant, and Matt spent the next few minutes spitting seeds for distance until the watermelon was nothing but green rinds. Mom passed around a grocery sack for the rinds and we all tossed our garbage in.

"Before we go," Dad said, "Brant, you took the first piece. Tell me how you felt carrying the whole watermelon on the hike."

"It was fine at first. Not too heavy." He flexed and I groaned while Axyl laughed. "But I wasn't complaining when I handed it off to Charlie."

"Would you bring one along on our next hike?"

"It was worth it to have it to eat at the end. If I didn't have to carry it by myself, I'd bring one again."

"So having others share the load was helpful?" Dad asked.

Brant shrugged. "Yeah. I guess so."

"This is a question for everyone and it isn't something you need to answer out loud. Is there something you are carrying by yourself- something from work, about a friend, with school starting in a few months, or inside your own mind- that would be easier to handle if you told someone else about it- a parent, a sibling, a friend? Think about that. Life throws us curve balls and that's why we have families.

We share the burden so our own isn't so heavy." Dad looked at me, Brant, and Bailey. "I want us to go around the circle and each say one word that represents an issue you could use help with. Mom and I will get with you in the next few days to find out how we can help you with it. Matt and Kristin, would you check with Axyl on the drive home?" Matt and Kristin nodded. "Charlie, you go first."

My eyes widened and the words caught in my throat. "Um…" What to say that wasn't too revealing? "Friends," I finally said. That was vague enough, but encompassed all the underlying issues.

Dad gave me a small smile and moved on to Brant. I was both excited and terrified of the conversation that would follow with my parents in the next few days. Dad had just unknowingly given me permission to help myself.

Chapter 16

A faint light roused me from sleep that night. I lay still, trying to figure out where the light was coming from. What time was it? I groped around for my phone, but couldn't find it. I went up on my elbow and looked across the room.

"What are you doing?" I demanded, groggily.

Bailey jumped and spun around, dropping her phone- the source of the light. "Nothing!" she hissed. "Go back to sleep."

My eyes gradually adjusted to the black night and I watched Bailey pause at the top of the stairs, glancing warily back at me before tiptoeing down, shoes in hand, and slinking out the side door like a specter.

I wanted to be impressed at how easy she made it look to sneak out of the house in the middle of the night, but my mind wouldn't allow me to dwell on it as questions rushed in. Was this the first time she'd snuck out? Where was she going? Was she meeting someone? Who? Why?

"Stupid Bailey," I muttered under my breath. I couldn't just let her go. Could I?

"No," I sighed, throwing back the covers and reaching for my navy hoodie. What if something happened to her and I could have stopped it?

I grabbed my shoes and silently floated down the stairs, slipping out the side door like Bailey had only seconds before. The deck was cool under my bare feet and I shivered in the chilly night, glad I had my hoodie. I tugged my shoes on and crept down the wooden stairs to the gravel driveway. I paused to look and listen. Seconds passed before I saw a small light bobbing down the road ahead. I'd have to go slowly so my feet on the road wouldn't alert Bailey that she was being followed. Where was she going?

A quarter of a mile later, I had my answer as a silhouette that looked remarkably identical to Axyl's tall, muscular form stepped out from the trees at the edge of the lake. My sister...and...Axyl?!

I stopped short. I knew it!

I wanted to look away from them, but I couldn't. It's that train wreck feeling where you can't pull your eyes away from the gruesome horror staring you in the face no matter how badly you want to.

Just then, the moon appeared between the clouds, bathing Bailey and Axyl in a soft light. He said something I couldn't hear as his hand reached for her.

I turned away as betrayal clawed at my heart.

I had never hated anyone, but in that moment, I hated Bailey.

Tears clogged my throat and blinded me, and I stumbled on the uneven ground, hurrying to get away from them in the faint moonlight.

My paradise came crashing down around me. My trees. My lake. My reprieve. They weren't mine anymore. They had been stolen from me. Ripped from my grasp in seconds. They were tainted by betrayal and lost wishes and dreams. I could never come here again without seeing *them.* Their clandestine rendezvous would haunt me and chip away at my broken heart every time I thought of it.

I looked back briefly to make sure I wasn't being followed and saw someone step out of the shadows near the cabin three doors down from ours. I picked up my pace, not wanting to find out who it was.

Gravel crunched behind me, and the fear of discovery gave way to a new kind of fear. I knew instinctively that it wasn't Axyl or Bailey behind me. I ran the remaining thirty yards to our cabin, but just as I raised my foot to scale the stairs, arms encircled my waist from behind and yanked me back with such force that we both went sprawling on the gravel.

Rocks bit into my bare legs and the air was forced from my lungs. I knew I'd feel the bruise on my hip in the morning if I lived through the panic of not being able to draw a breath. An act that was usually involuntary became all I could think about. I sputtered and finally sucked in a desperate breath, willing my lungs to reinflate.

"You should have taken my gift," a man whispered fiercely in my ear. "But you dropped it in the dirt. I see how you are."

Gift? In the dirt?

The other day with creepy Josh, the notebook and the rope swing flashed through my mind. When I realized who it was that held me, I was angry.

Who did he think he was?

No way was I letting him get away with yanking me from my cabin. If he thought I'd go with him quietly, he was mistaken. I wasn't good with people, but even I knew when to talk.

Or scream.

"Help!" I screamed at the top of my lungs. If Bailey and Axyl were close, they would help me, right?

Josh clamped a hand over my mouth. I tried to bite his fingers, but his hand was too tight. I was suffocating, but this time with my lungs full. Like pinching off a balloon, only muffled squeaks escaped around his disgusting hand.

I kicked and struggled against him, dragging my feet through the gravel to stop our progress. He lifted me in the air and I kicked backward, trying to connect with anything substantial.

"Hey!" Axyl yelled from behind us. Relief washed over me.

Josh looked back and swore. Like a wuss, he threw me to the ground and ran. A real man would've stayed there and taken it. Instead, Axyl had to chase after him while yelling at Bailey to call the police. I watched from my cold, uncomfortable seat on the ground as, like a scene from a movie, Axyl leapt through the air and landed on Josh's back, knocking him to the ground with an "umph."

How does it feel to deflate, Josh? I wondered, rubbing my chest.

Josh fought back, but I'm sure I've mentioned how athletic Axyl is.

By the time the red and blue flashing lights rounded the last bend leading to our cabin, Bailey was beside me and Axyl had pinned a now-unconscious Josh to the ground.

That gravel bites, eh Josh?

A kind policeman took statements from each of us while a few curious vacationers from cabins along the road peeked out their windows and stood on their porches in their pajamas for clues about their interrupted sleep.

"Do you need me to call an EMT?" Officer Nicols asked, briefly looking me and Axyl over.

I glanced down at the scrapes on my legs and ankles and shook my head. They were scratches, really.

"You're very brave," Officer Nichols said to me as his partner loaded a groggy, handcuffed Josh into the patrol car.

I shrugged. It hadn't occurred to me to be afraid. All I could think of while Josh was trying to drag me into the trees was that he'd picked the wrong night to get in my way. I was already mad and heartbroken about Bailey and Axyl. I wanted to rip into someone and I was glad it could be Josh.

I keep to myself. I mind my own business. Why couldn't people just leave me alone?

Technically, my anger at Axyl and Bailey had probably saved me. But I wouldn't be thanking them anytime soon for the circumstances that dragged me from the cabin in the first place. Their saving my life didn't wipe out past wrongs. It just put them on hold temporarily.

"There are people you can talk to about what happened if you feel like you need to," the police officer told me. "I can call you in the morning with contact information."

I nodded. "Thank you."

"I think you should tell your parents," Axyl said, squeezing my shoulder as we watched the police car drive away until the darkness swallowed it up.

"I'd rather just forget it happened," I replied, suddenly exhausted. "Thank you, by the way."

He wrapped an arm around my shoulders in a side hug.

"Are you okay?" I asked him, worried he'd hurt himself saving me.

He glanced down at his right hand, but answered, "I'm fine." He paused, then said, "I'm glad we came along when we did. Can you imagine…" His arm tightened around my shoulders.

No. I didn't want to imagine it.

"I didn't know it was you at first," he said.

"Why were you even out here?" Bailey asked. Then a thought must have occurred to her. "Were you meeting Josh?" She had the nerve to look scandalized.

Axyl's arm fell from my shoulders, and he and Bailey regarded me with different expressions. Bailey's, I could read, while Axyl's, I couldn't. His almost looked like disappointment. But for what, I couldn't imagine.

"If you don't tell Mom and Dad," Bailey said, "I will."

Were her words out of concern for me, or did she think I'd get in trouble? Bailey never concerned herself about me, so I figured it was the latter. I wouldn't have been outside if it wasn't for her. I knew it was stupid to be outside alone in the middle of the night. What happened with Josh had not been my fault. It's not like I'd encouraged him.

I wondered how Bailey would explain her and Axyl's quick response to my emergency when no one else in our cabin heard anything, but I didn't bring it up. It took all my concentration to lift one foot up the steps in front of the other.

Bailey hurried ahead of us, but stopped short when the cabin door opened before she could turn the knob. Like so many others, my parents hadn't slept through it.

"Was that a police car outside?" my dad asked.

"Yes," I answered wearily.

"What happened?" Mom asked.

"You'll probably want to sit down," I said, sinking into the couch. "There's a guy who lives three cabins down…"

Forty-five minutes later, my parents had asked all the questions they could think of. I knew there would be more, but for now, my sore and tired body was grateful they were talked out.

I left Bailey and my parents in the living room, not envying them the conversation they were about to have about why Bailey was outside, and I slowly climbed the stairs to the loft. The satisfaction I felt at the thought that finally some of the consequences for Bailey's poor choices had caught up with her lasted half a second before the pain and exhaustion settled back in and I buried my face in my pillow and cried myself to sleep.

Innocence
Ripped away,
Stolen.
Taking what was never yours to take.
Snatched away,
Robbed.
Extracting forbidden pieces.
Sharp rocks cutting- inside and out.
Rusted metal slicing- mind and body.
Mended,
Reclaiming those lost pieces.

Healed,
Recovering what most needs to be recovered.
I never relinquished my soul.

                    -The Skinny Tomboy

Chapter 17

"Hey, Charlie," Brant hollered up the stairs to the loft the next morning. "We're going to the lake. Come on."

I raised my pen to my mouth and closed my eyes. No way was I going to the lake with Axyl.

"No thanks," I called back.

"No?" Brant questioned as his feet stomped up the stairs. "We're going to the lake," he repeated as if I hadn't heard him the first time.

"I know. I heard you."

"Then put the notebook away and come on. Axyl wants to go one more time before they leave."

"I'm good," I replied, lowering the pen to the page again.

Brant stepped farther into the loft. "You don't want to go to the lake?" He frowned. "What's going on?"

"Nothing, Brant. I just don't want to go."

His hands went to his hips. "You never turn down the lake, Charlie. Is it because of last night?"

Yes. But not for the reason he thought.

"There's a first time for everything," I said.

One of his brows rose in surprise. "Sarcasm too? Now I know something's wrong."

"Nothing's wrong, Brant," I said, my voice rising in irritation. Why couldn't he drop it and leave me alone in my misery?

"If it's not about your midnight smack down with the pedophile..."

Leave it to Brant to tell it like it is. No sugar coating. To some, it may be off-putting, but I'd rather be open about it than have everyone walk on eggshells around the topic. Besides, I knew his ability to talk about it might make it seem like he didn't think it was a big deal, but I'd heard him talking with Mom and Dad about it this morning and he hadn't been happy. If his ranting and shouting hadn't convinced me he was furious on my behalf, his muttered threats and oaths had.

I think it's a good thing Axyl jumped Josh. I'm not sure what Josh would look like today if Brant had been the one to catch him.

While I was busy processing Brant, he was still trying to figure me out.

"It's got to be about…Hm…" Brant was quiet for a moment, then he chuckled. "It's because *he's* leaving, huh? The love of Charlie's young life is leaving and she'll never see him again. Boo hoo. Her heart is broken." He laughed again, certain he was right.

I glared at Brant. "Shut up, Brant. You don't know anything," I muttered.

"I would if you'd tell me." He watched me, frowning. "If you really liked him, seems like you'd want to spend as much time with him as possible before he leaves."

"Then that should be your clue that I don't like him," I bit out.

"I'll never understand girls," he grumbled. "Just quit with all the 'poor me' stuff and come on."

"I'm not going," I said slowly, enunciating each word.

Brant turned in a huff. "Sorry, Axyl," he said in a loud voice as he descended the stairs. "Charlie's sick. Or she's being lame."

"She doesn't want to go to the lake?" came Axyl's astonished reply. "I mean, last night was pretty scary," he amended.

I didn't hear Brant's response as they left the cabin, the screen door slamming behind them.

Let them think I was lame. Let them think I was sick. I *was* sick! Sick of Axyl. Sick of boys and their stupid, confusing games. Sick that I'd let myself think someone like Axyl could ever like me. Even someone like Josh didn't like me. He was just twisted. And I was sick that I'd let myself like someone I'd never see again.

Why would anyone do that? It was just asking for suffering.

I lowered my face to my bed and released the tears that threatened when Brant begged me to go to my sanctuary and I had to tell him no.

•••••

"Charlie! Bailey! They're leaving," Mom hollered up the stairs a few hours later. "Come down and say goodbye."

I felt another painful tug at my heart at my mother's words and willed my tears away.

Bailey and I had been in the loft, together but separate, for most of the day. I couldn't look at her or I would cry again. Then she'd ask if I was crying over what happened with Josh when really it was because I knew about her late night meeting with Axyl.

But I shouldn't have worried she'd notice me. She was more subdued than I'd ever seen her. I wondered how she'd talked her way out of being outside with Axyl last night. She'd probably lied and said the cop car lights woke her like they did everyone else.

Even if she was in trouble, for someone in love, she sure didn't act like it. She should be smiling and giggling; spending every possible minute left with Axyl. I didn't understand her at all.

Bailey stood from her bed, eyeing me. "Aren't you going down to say goodbye to *Axyl*?" she asked. The way she said his name ticked me off. She already had him. Did she have to rub it in? But that was her way. She loved to hate me.

I didn't say anything. Instead, I chewed on my pen, hoping the words that evaded me would somehow spill out onto the paper and take my sadness with them.

"I'll never understand you," Bailey muttered and clomped down the stairs.

Oh, well. I'd never understand her either.

"Chaaaarlie!" My mother's voice reached up the stairs. This time it was more insistent.

I knew if I didn't go down, she'd march up to the loft and drag me down, lecturing about good manners all the way. I'm not six.

My resigned sigh was more of a growl and I peeled myself off my bed. Taking the elastic from my wrist, I threw my hair up in a ponytail and straightened my day-old t-shirt.

Who cared what I looked like? I'd never see these people again. The thought made my eyes glisten and I swallowed hard.

"How are you feeling?" Mom asked. She was waiting for me at the bottom of the stairs, one foot poised above the first tread. Any other day, I would have smiled that I knew her so well.

"I'm fine," I replied tightly.

"I thought you would have been the first one out there telling them goodbye," my mom said, following me to the door. "You and Axyl seemed to get along really well." Her tone of voice hinted at a knowing smile I was glad I couldn't see.

I scoffed. "Not well enough."

"Why? What happened?"

I didn't answer because we were on the porch in front of everyone. And if Bailey hadn't told them about meeting up with Axyl last night, I wasn't going to be the one to inform them.

I put on a fake smile and stomped down the stairs, knowing I probably looked ridiculous with my face and body so at odds with each other.

I didn't have to look to know where Axyl was. I could feel him. That pull that I felt from him was still there, but I didn't understand it any more now than I did before I'd witnessed the meeting at the lake last night. Yesterday, I thought it meant something, like there was a chance he liked me too. Ha! Today, I know how stupid I was and that he is in love with my little sister.

I focused on my feet taking me closer to Kristin and Matt instead of lifting my face for everyone to see the hurt written all over it.

"Oh, Charlie," Kristin said, pulling me in for a hug. "It was so good to see you again. You are such a beautiful young woman. I'm glad for the chance to get to know you better."

"It was good to see you too, Mrs. Stewart. Fully clothed this time."

Brant snorted somewhere near me, but I didn't look at him.

Matt put an arm around my shoulders and gave me an awkward squeeze. "Thanks for putting up with us, Charlie. This is a nice place you got here."

"Well, you are welcome anytime," Mom said, turning and wrapping her arms around Kristin. "I'm so glad you could come."

"We need to do this more often," Kristin replied, returning her hug.

No, I silently begged. At least not if I have to be there. I couldn't handle seeing Axyl again. But what if he was at school and couldn't go. Would that be worse than having him show up?

"You're quiet," Axyl whispered, coming up next to me, bumping me with his shoulder. My body wanted to sigh and lean into him. Why did he have to smell so good? "I mean, more quiet than usual. And where's your notebook?" He took a step back and studied me. I immediately missed his solid warmth. "It's understandable because of last night. But you skipped out on the lake today. I never thought I'd see that. Are you sick?" he wanted to know.

I shook my head, but didn't say anything.

"I didn't think you were coming down to say goodbye." He nudged me again with his shoulder. When I didn't respond or even look at him, he asked, "Are you mad at me?"

That got my attention.

"Why would I be mad at you?" I managed. Although I could think of one very big reason to be furious.

He shrugged. "I don't know. I mean," he lowered his voice, "Before everything happened last night, I was at the lake."

My brows lifted in surprise. He would bring that up? Seriously? He'd really bring that up?

What a jerk!

Wait. Did he know I had followed Bailey to the lake? That I had seen them? Had he seen me peeping at them from the bushes? Did they do something he thinks Bailey told me about? Is it because he's nineteen and she's only fifteen and he doesn't want to get in trouble because he and my little sister were messing around?

"You are not the person I thought you were," I ground out, finding the anger lodged deep beneath the heartache and betrayal. In fact, he made me sick. I was glad he was leaving and I'd never have to see him again.

Confusion pulled his dark brows down. "Huh?" He reached for my arm, but all I saw was him reaching for Bailey in the moonlight. I jerked back and turned for the cabin. "Charlie?" he called after me.

But I was so done. I'd said my goodbyes and now I was walking away.

"Not even a goodbye hug," Bailey commented smugly, passing me on the porch.

Nope. I didn't want him to touch me let alone wrap his arms around me.

I let the screen door slam behind me, not caring that my mother's chiding voice followed the bang of the door. I wasn't about to stick around and watch Bailey get her goodbye hug.

I may not be smart when it comes to boys and love, but I wasn't *that* stupid.

Love
A carefree laugh
wrenching.
A soft touch
white hot.
A meaningful look
piercing.
A euphoric feeling
ravenous.
An infantile heart
extinct.
How can I mourn what was never mine?
-The Skinny Tomboy

Hours. The Stewarts had been gone for hours. And I'd felt every lonely one.

As soon as I'd heard the car doors slam and the crunch of tires on gravel, I'd slipped down from the loft and out the side door to the lake for comfort.

Now, hours later, only the darkness and thoughts of men lurking in shadows pushed me back to the cabin.

Not even the lake and my notebook could ease the pain. How had I ever found comfort in them before? They were a sorry substitute for a touch on my hand or an arm around my shoulders. Heck, I'd even take a teasing laugh if it meant he was still here.

I squeezed my eyes shut as the feeling of being wrapped around Axyl's warm body at the lake days ago invaded my thoughts.

I quickly pushed him out, only to have him replaced by the memory of my desperate actions at the lake this afternoon after he and his family were long gone. Every movement of the dock, every voice, had me glancing up, hoping. How had I gotten used to him being right behind me in so short a time?

Why hadn't I talked to him, asked him, when I'd had the chance?

I knew why. Because I'd been afraid of the answer. I'd been afraid that what I'd known all along- that no one could ever like me, especially over Bailey- was true. But that didn't matter so much now. If

145

he was standing in front of me this minute, I'd ask him about meeting up with Bailey in the dark.

I slowly climbed the stairs to the loft, ignoring my mom's question about missing dinner and did I want any. I didn't.

"What are you doing?" I asked Bailey, rushing across the loft and yanking my notebook out of her hand. "How many times do I have to tell you to leave my stuff alone?"

"I thought you had to be missing Axyl by now. I was looking for clues in your little book about how much."

"I don't care about Axyl!" I cried in exasperation.

"Not enough to put anything about him in your dumb book. It's full of words that don't make any sense. Anyone could write a bunch of words on paper. You call that poetry?" she snorted. Funny, Axyl had accused me of the exact same thing. They really were so much alike.

My chest rose and fell rapidly when I noticed the papers littering the floor. My poems, parts of me. She'd torn them out? I frantically fell to my knees and began gathering them piece by piece. I wanted to scream. This time she had gone too far.

I angrily snatched up another piece, shoving it under my arm with the rest, and glared up at her. Her laughter mocked me from my powerless position at her feet.

"What's the matter, Charles? Upset you didn't get your goodbye hug? Mine was nice." Her venomous smile told me all I needed to know about her and Axyl. "You should have stuck around. Maybe he would have given you one too."

Her words taunted me and fire should have been shooting from my eyes with the hatred that emanated from them.

"Go on, Charles. Say it," she goaded. I snatched up another poem from the floor and shoved it under my arm.

"Just say it!" Bailey said, her voice rising in frustration.

"Say what?" I asked through gritted teeth.

"Say what you want to say." She was getting more angry by the second. I could tell because it mirrored my own emotions.

"If you know what I want to say, Bailey, then why don't you tell me?" I spat.

"I hate you!" she screamed and I reared back on my knees, stunned. The movement made me lose my balance and I sat hard on my butt on the floor. The bent and crumpled pages landed next to me in a tangled mix of words I couldn't say. I could only feel them. And right now, if I could pick up my pen, I would write words like shocked, stunned, amazed, distressed.

I mean, I know we don't get along. There's really no love lost between us. But to actually hear the words coming from her laughing mouth hurt. It surprised me how much they hurt.

Bruised. Defeated. Lost.

"Come on, Charles. You can do it. You want to say, 'I hate you'. Say it."

She wanted a fight. She was egging me on.

"Why won't you say it, Charlie? Why don't you ever tell anyone how you feel? You walk around like you have this superior stick up your butt with all the answers to the universe locked in your brain or in that stupid notebook you carry everywhere with you, and no one knows how you feel about anything. You. Never. Talk."

"What? I talk."

"When?" Bailey demanded. "To who?"

The correct term is to *whom*, but I figured now wouldn't be the greatest time to tell her that.

"I talk to Mom," I defended. "I talk to Brant."

"So it's just me you don't talk to. It's just me you hate."

I laughed bitterly. "You don't *want* me to talk to you. All you ever do is tell me how terrible I look. You ruin my stuff." I held out a torn page of my poetry as evidence. "You find any excuse to make fun of me or put me down. Why would I willingly seek out someone who treats me that way? *You* hate *me*, but are projecting your hate on me so you have one more thing to blame me for."

Bailey swallowed hard and deflated before my eyes. "How else can I get Mom and Dad's attention?" she asked softly, a little of the fight retreating. Her head was down and she studied her nails.

"What?" I asked in confusion.

"How else can I get their attention?" she repeated, meeting my eyes. "You are the perfect daughter, the perfect child. You do everything Mom asks, and then some, just to make me look bad. You get straight A's and you don't have to work for them. You're the president of every nerd club at school. You know everything about everything. Do you know how hard it is..." Tears formed in her beautiful eyes and they became dark crystal pools until her anguish spilled over and rolled silently down her cheeks. Meanwhile, my own eyes were likely to pop out of my head with each sentence she uttered. Disbelief was not a strong enough noun to describe my feelings at her revelations.

And she continued. "...to watch disappointment fill my teacher's eyes when they realize I'm not a carbon copy of you? I live in your shadow everyday!" She flung a hand at me. "You have this long, lean body that all the girls at school are jealous of, and a style no one could begin to copy because there's no continuity to it."

Continuity. "Good word choice, by the way," I quickly interjected.

Bailey threw her hands in the air and screeched. "Only you, Charlie! Only you would pause in the middle of an argument to compliment someone on their vocabulary. You drive me crazy!"

"And you drive me crazy," I admitted. And it felt good to say it out loud.

But I guess she wasn't finished listing all my imaginary exemplary traits because she continued as if she hadn't heard me confess that she made me crazy every day of our lives.

"You don't care what anyone thinks. All the boys drool when you walk down the hall and you are clueless. You have no idea how hard I worked the past two weeks to get Axyl to pay me the slightest bit of attention. He was with you every second. And when he wasn't with you, he was asking about you- 'What does she like? What doesn't she like? What does she write in her notebook? Is she seeing anyone? How does she feel about long distance relationships?'" Bailey threw her hands in the air. And my eyes were seriously bugging out by now! Were we talking about the same Axyl? Because he gave no indication, no hint, nada, nothing. He was the one who said it's dumb to get involved with someone right before leaving for school.

"Even Josh wanted you," Bailey said, sitting down hard on her bed.

Was that supposed to make me feel good? Did his attention equate to some kind of accomplishment on my part in her mind? Did she not hear me tell the police and our parents how the lunatic attacked me from behind? I never wanted his attention.

"I saw you two at the lake last night," I accused. "You and Axyl."

"That explains why you were outsi- Wait. You followed me?" she asked in disbelief.

"You were acting more weird than normal. I thought you were sneaking out to meet...I don't know...Josh or someone equally as dangerous." I shuddered remembering his vise-like arms around my middle. "Contrary to what you think, I don't hate you. I couldn't let you go alone if you were going to be murdered. Or worse."

"You are so dramatic," she informed me with a roll of her eyes."

"Takes one to know one."

"So you saw how Axyl completely blew me off as soon as he saw I wasn't you?" Bailey asked.

"Why would he have expected me?" I questioned.

Bailey clammed up and studied her manicure again. Guilt was not her best color.

I became suspicious.

"What did you do, Bailey?!"

"I only...I was trying...Fine! I told him to give me his number so I could give it to you. He's so painfully shy when it comes to girls, *I* feel awkward *for* him."

Were we talking about the same Axyl?

She continued, "Then I pretended to be you later when I texted him to meet me at the lake. It was my failed last ditch attempt to get him to notice me."

I moved closer. "What happened?" Despite myself, I was totally into this story. I should be angry because Bailey lied to Axyl and used me to get him.

"As soon as he saw it was me, he was like, 'Bailey? What are you doing out here? Do you know what time it is?'" She snorted. "Like I can't tell time. I told him of course I knew what time it was and that I was meeting someone. He wanted to know who. He went all big brother on me- like Brant. It never crossed his mind that I was there to meet *him*. That alone told me how he felt about me. Or about you, I guess. That made me mad, of course, because everyone always likes you..." She waved a dismissive hand. "Add to that, that he treated me like a baby... so I told him I was there to meet Josh." She cringed.

"Josh?" I asked, knowing she couldn't possibly be talking about the same Josh who attacked me.

"Yes. The same Josh who tried to kill you last night." Bailey said. I wasn't sure because I'd never seen it on Bailey before, but she almost looked embarrassed that she'd used Josh to lie to Axyl; especially after the way the night had ended.

I groaned. "You know him? Baiiiiley. Please don't tell me you've met him somewhere before." Fear for her crawled up my throat. What if he'd grabbed Bailey last night instead of me?

Bailey scoffed. "Give me a little credit, Charlie. I don't think bathing is a regular part of his daily routine."

"You've been close enough to him to *smell* him?" I asked, horrified.

"You don't have to be closer than ten feet to smell him. Trust me." She waved a hand in front of her face, her cute nose scrunched in disgust. "I'm sorry you were."

I didn't remember him being particularly ripe last night. Maybe I'd caught him on a good day. That was something to be grateful for. But I hadn't been in the frame of mind to notice something like that anyway.

Regardless, ten feet was still too close for me, but I was more relieved that she hadn't done something stupid with him to say anything else about proximity.

"Anyway..." Bailey drawled, turning the topic away from Josh. I was more than okay with that. "After Axyl gave his opinion about Josh, blah, blah, blah..." She rolled her eyes. "I asked him what he was doing there. He said he couldn't sleep, so he went down there to think. He played it off pretty well, but you should have seen the look he gave our cabin."

I put my hand on her arm, so caught up in her answer that I was unaware I was touching her. "What did he look like?" I had to know. I was eating this up- any morsel she was willing to throw my way.

"Hot. Really hot. Well, you saw him. He was wearing-"

"No, Bailey!" I snapped. "Not, what did he *look* like? What was his facial expression, his body language? What was the look on his face when he stared at our cabin?" I wanted to shake her. I'm not a violent person. What was happening to me?

"Oh, right. Sorry. Like he was so disappointed and his heart was breaking."

"No he didn't!" I whispered. "We're talking about the same Axyl, right?"

Bailey nodded solemnly and drew an X over her heart with her finger. "I promise. Besides, how many Axyl's do you know?"

"Good point. Okay. So what happened next?"

"He said he'd planned to hang around for a while, but he'd walk me back to the cabin instead."

Thank heaven for that. If he hadn't, who knows what would have happened to me.

"I told him he didn't need to do that," Bailey continued. "I'm a big girl and could make it on my own. But he said he wasn't going to let me meet Josh in the dark at the lake only to get back to school and hear on the news that my ravished body- and he really used the word ravished. I mean, who talks like that? Well, except you- he didn't want to hear about my body washing up on the shore of the lake weeks later." She paused in her retelling to say, "Is that what my English teacher meant by irony?" She waved the thought away. "I think Axyl really just wanted to walk toward the cabin to see if we ran into you."

I rolled my eyes. "Whatever."

"You don't believe me?"

"No. I believe you about everything except how into me you think Axyl is."

"Well, you better believe it. He's totally gone."

"Don't remind me," I moaned.

"No. Not *gone* gone. Gone as in he's going back to school and when he looks at any other girl, he'll only see you. I give him a week tops before he texts you."

"With what number?" I asked, raising a brow and my phone. "You gave him your number, not mine."

Bailey gave me a secretive smile. "Trust me."

And for the first time in...well, ever, I wanted to believe her. So badly.

"You know, Bailey. This is not how I saw this summer playing out."

"You saw me doing something stupid like running away with Josh the serial rapist." At the look on my face, she said, "You can admit it. You think I'm really that stupid, don't you?"

"I hope you wouldn't be. But come on. We have never gotten along. You are totally into boys. You act rashly quite often."

"I don't even know what 'rashly' means. So how can I act that way?"

"Never mind. Let's just say I'm so glad you didn't meet Josh at the lake or anywhere else. And...tell me how it would be possible that Axyl would contact me." Yes. I had stooped that low.

Bailey laughed. "There are *some* secrets I'll never reveal."

"Unlike me who reveals no secrets what-so-ever?"

Bailey shrugged and remained silent.

I sighed. "It's what I do- the poetry notebook. When you hit puberty and were on permanent PMS, our tenuous relationship became nonexistent. I heard writing helps people work through feelings. Rather than take my anger and frustration out on you, I wrote. I didn't realize how silent I've become until you pointed it out. Since I 'talked' through the poetry, I didn't have to talk out loud."

"That's not healthy. You know that, right?" Bailey pointed out. "You don't have any friends. You don't communicate regularly with the family. I mean, your writing is good, but come out and visit the world once in a while. It's nice out here."

"I know. I love it here. Don't you?"

"Honestly? No."

My head jerked up in surprise. "You don't like coming to the lake every summer? First Brant and now you."

"It's because you are the favorite child," Bailey pouted.

"That's not true," I argued. I didn't want it to be true. How could I be so selfish and self-absorbed?!

"If you could go anywhere for summer break, where would you go?" I asked.

Bailey's face lit up like I'd never seen it do. "I've always wanted to spend weeks on either coast. Find out if what they say is true- that the Pacific really is warmer than the Atlantic."

I snorted. "I should have known it would be somewhere you could show off your body."

"What does that mean?" Bailey demanded, sounding surprisingly offended. "I can show off my body at the lake too, remember?"

"That swimming suit? The new one?" I scrunched up my nose. "Really, Bailey?"

"Getting attention is getting attention," she said with a shrug.

"Okay. I get it. So the coast is more than skimpy bathing suits to you." I paused and studied her for a moment. "Who do you want to be, Bailey?"

"I...I want to be like you. But without the poetry. And with better clothes. And friends."

"You said you liked my clothes."

"No...I said you have a style no one can duplicate."

"So you *don't* like my clothes?"

"Would you be open to a few suggestions?" Her eyes scrunched at the corners like she was afraid she'd offend me.

"Maybe," I hedged, feeling my heart start to pound.

She gave me a fierce look.

I counted to ten in my head before releasing a breath. "Fine. But Bailey, you're good as you are. Find yourself. You don't have to be exactly like me."

She snorted. "Tell that to every teacher at Ridgemont High."

"You don't have to be exactly like anyone except yourself," I insisted. "Find out who you want to be and be the best of that person."

"I will," she promised. "But you find yourself too, Charlie."

I was working on that.

And though I knew it was a tenuous one, I offered Bailey a small smile to show her that I would also work on our evolving relationship.

Smoke and Mirrors
Looking in the mirror
Reflections skew.
Reflections palter.
Reflections dissemble.
Looking past the mirror
I never saw myself until today.
                              -Charlie

Chapter 18

"Mom sent me to get you," Brant said, plopping down beside me on the dock the next evening. "Dinner's ready."

Okay," I responded, distracted. "Thanks."

"Well, at least I got a thanks this time." He stood to leave and I tugged him back down.

"Wait a sec, Brant. Am I self-absorbed? Selfish?"

"Uh, well…"

I groaned and closed my notebook. "You hesitated. It's true."

"You're not self-absorbed the way Bailey is self-absorbed. It's more like you retreat to this place in your mind that only you know and only you can go. And you like it that way. The No Trespassing sign is neon with barbs and vicious attack dogs and stuff."

"Convincing imagery."

He shrugged. "You asked."

"You're right. I did. Thank you for being honest with me." I paused, moistening my lips and gathering my courage. "You're leaving at the end of the summer, huh?" The thought made me sick. Home wouldn't be the same without him. I dreaded it. And I dreaded how things would change between us. So I never talked about it with him. If I didn't say it, it wasn't happening.

But I'd promised Bailey.

"Yeah. I know we have good schools in Utah, but I want to see things."

"You've sacrificed 'seeing things' this summer so I could come here. Even though it's your last summer at home, you chose to spend it somewhere you hate. For me."

"I don't *hate* it here," Brant said. "I can just think of a lot of other places I'd like to see instead of this place year after year."

I lowered my eyes. "I'm sorry, Brant."

"Don't apologize, Charlie. This summer has been the best one we've spent here in a long time with Axyl and-"

"-Iris," I suggested, swallowing a grin.

"I was going to say Coleman and everyone." But he was fighting a grin himself, so I knew better. "Like I said," he continued. "I don't *hate* it."

"But you don't *love* it either."

"No one could love it as much as you love it." He bumped me with his shoulder.

I nodded slowly. "Maybe." We were quiet for a time, then I said, "You're a good brother."

"I know. Can I go?" he asked.

I smiled. He'd have to work up to this 'conversation with people' thing too. "Yup. You mind if I walk back with you?"

I could tell he was surprised by my request, but he stood and held a hand down to me anyway.

"Something weird is going on here since the Stewarts left," he observed.

"Define weird," I encouraged.

"Bailey is suddenly different. You're wanting to interact with people." He shook his head. "Weird."

"It's okay, Brant." I patted him on the back. "You're still my favorite sibling. Just don't tell Bailey. It might hurt her feelings."

He peered down at me like I had been overtaken by an alien life form, and repeated, "Weird."

•••••

"I have something to say," I announced during our otherwise quiet dinner.

Four sets of eyes focused on me. Utter silence. It kind of made me want to laugh. How had I never noticed our lack of interaction. It was just as Brant had said.

Instead of laughing, I settled for a smile and said, "I was wondering if we could cut our time at the lake short to go somewhere else for the rest of the summer?"

Four different expressions greeted my question/suggestion: Curiosity, concern, hope, and pride.

My dad set his fork down, eyeing me closely. "You love this place. Why would you want to leave early?" He and Mom shared a look. "Is this about that man the other night? Because if it is, we can call and get you an appointment to see someone when we get home."

"It's not about that, Dad," I said.

"Honey, if this is about Axyl, he's on the other side of the country. He's in college and you're still in high school," my mom reminded me unnecessarily. I barely refrained from giving an annoyed roll of my eyes when her comment elicited a snort from Brant.

"I know it might not be possible to go somewhere else since staying here costs us next to nothing, and going somewhere else would require money we hadn't planned on. I just wondered if it might be a possibility." When no one said anything, I tried again. "We could discuss it for next year then? Open mic time. You know, brainstorming."

My parents exchanged a look as Brant drummed excitedly on the table and Bailey, well...I didn't look at her. I couldn't decide if she would think I was doing this for her and Brant as proof I was finding my best self or to tip the scales on the 'favorite child' theory.

"I've always wanted to go to either coast," Bailey spoke softly.

I shot her a grateful smile that I hoped also looked encouraging.

"At this point, we're closer to the West Coast," Brant added. "But I'd be okay with a road trip." His drumming crescendoed and he stood with his plate in hand. He squeezed my shoulder on the way to the kitchen sink, then joined us back at the table.

"West Coast, then?" my dad asked, looking at each of us in turn. I could see his excitement in the way his eyes crinkled at the edges and he shifted with new energy in his chair.

That made me happy.

And who knows, I might find another favorite place. I could start a list of favorites. I already had the notebook.

The Offering
A vessel, heavy and empty.
A word.
A gesture.
A thought.
A vessel, weightless and overflowing.
                    -Charlie

Epilogue

I felt my phone buzz in my pocket and rolled my eyes. It was most likely Bailey gushing about yet another hot guy in one of her classes. I had gotten four or five texts a day from her the first week of school. It had slowed to two or three every other day now that she'd met practically every guy in the school. Plus, she thinks my compulsive need to check my phone when it buzzes is hilarious because it makes me break a school rule: No phones in class. And since I don't break school rules, she texts ridiculous nonsense like 'at' or 'the' so she can laugh as she pictures me breaking the rules yet again. I never text her back, but she knows I'm checking.

I'm not sure yet if our fragile truce has had a positive or negative effect on me. My therapist thinks it's good, and she's the professional, so I'll keep working at it.

And speaking of therapists, I'm still working on my fear of change. Brant would be home from school this weekend to visit and I couldn't wait. He'd probably spend more time with old high school friends, but I'd take whatever time I could get.

Maybe I'd tag along.

When my phone buzzed again, I ground my teeth and sighed. I pulled it out and hid it under my desk, glancing at Mr. Kimball to make sure his back was turned. His love affair with chemistry equations appeared to still be going strong.

Bailey: Any interesting texts lately?
Me: Besides yours?
Bailey: Ha ha. Yes
Me: No. Should I?

I felt my phone buzz again and glanced at Mr. Kimball to make sure the coast was clear before looking down at it, expecting to see Bailey's reply.

Instead of a text from Bailey, it was from a number I didn't recognize. Not Brant then either. And the wording was strangely specific.

Unknown: Can you tell me how I can get a hold of a certain skinny tomboy?

I think I choked because my friend, Avery, looked over at me with concern. "You okay?" she mouthed.

I nodded and pointed to my phone. She returned my nod and faced forward, never taking her eyes off Mr. Kimball. She'd be my lookout. I was grateful she had my back.

Avery's a nerd- as Bailey affectionately dubbed us- like me. We've had almost every class together since the beginning of our school career. I look back now and wonder why I never made an effort to be her friend before. She's the best. I never knew what I was missing. That thought made me sad and I promised myself that I'd thank Bailey for helping me see myself better.

But not in a text.

Text!

I looked down at my phone again. My heart was racing faster than...oh, who cares what it was racing like! It was beating out of my chest.

Me: Who is this?

Unknown: I was trying to stay awake during another boring college lecture and suddenly I was thinking about a lake

I smiled. Wide. Huge.

Me: Sounds nice. Any lake in particular?

Unknown: Yeah. I spent some time there this summer. I can't stop thinking about it

Me: Then you should know there is no skinny tomboy anymore

Unknown: ...

Unknown: That's too bad

Unknown: ...

Unknown: It was worth a shot

My stomach clenched at what sounded like him giving up. He didn't understand my words because he hadn't seen my inner transformation. My thumbs flew over the keys as I typed.

Me: No. Wait! There's Charlie. Just...Charlie

I closed my eyes and crossed my fingers that it was enough. That *I* was enough.

Unknown: …

Unknown: :) Hey, Charlie. This is Axyl

Soundtrack for the Book

https://open.spotify.com/track/0ABHhxQTaluB94ohp2RLSr?si=x
U_6UEWRQ8OLbGGFIzqurQ&utm_source=copy-link

Sunrise, Sunburn, Sunset- Luke Bryan, 2017
Feelin' It- Scotty McCreery, 2013
Goodbye Summer- Danielle Bradbery, 2018
Faded- Alan Walker, 2015
The One That Got Away- Jake Owen, 2011
What If I Never Get Over You- Lady Antebellum, 2019
Irreplaceable- Madilyn Paige, 2015
We Are Tonight- Billy Currington, 2013
Every Girl in this Town-Trisha Yearwood, 2019
Have It All- Jason Mraz, 2018
Nothin' Like You- Dan + Shay, 2014
19 You + Me- Dan + Shay, 2014
This Ones For The Girls- Martina McBride, 2003
Born To Fly- Sara Evans, 2000
You Say- Lauren Daigle, 2018
Who Says- Selena Gomez, 2011
(Ghost) Riders In The Sky- Johnny Cash, 1979
Kumbaya My Lord- Peter, Paul, and Mary, 1998

Discussion Questions

1. Charlie doesn't like being judged, but she is quick to judge and categorize others. Why is it dangerous to make a blanket judgment about people because of their looks? How does pride factor into this? Think of a time your opinion of a person changed once you looked past the surface and got to know them. Why is it important to be sensitive and nonjudgmental with people?

2. This story focuses a lot on passing judgment and selfishness. Which character in the story do you think would win an award for being the most judgemental? The most selfish? Why are these two characteristics destructive? How is making a judgment call different from being judgemental? How can you prevent selfishness in your own character?

3. What evidences do you see throughout the story that Charlie is evolving?

4. Charlie suffers from anxiety. Do you or anyone you know suffer from this condition? What do you do to combat it? How could you help a person with anxiety?

5. Charlie uses poetry as an outlet for her thoughts and feelings. What constructive outlet do you use when you are feeling strong emotions?

6. Bailey accuses Charlie of using her poetry to hide from the world physically and emotionally. Do you think that's true? At what point do outlets become a crutch? How can you prevent that from happening?

7. Brant's main job as a big brother is to smooth the way for Charlie through life. But Charlie wonders if he's been lying to her. What does she mean? Is Brant's protection better or worse than Bailey's honesty?

8. Charlie and Bailey don't have the best relationship, but Charlie and Brant do. What differences do you see in each

relationship that make them the way they are? How are your relationships with family? Regardless of where your relationships are, what steps could you take to strengthen them? Does strengthening the relationship mean you need to be each other's best friend?

9. A few times in the story, Brant pushed Charlie to do something hard. Was that a good or a bad way to make her face her fears?

10. What is one thing about yourself that you'd like to change? What is keeping you from changing? What small step could you take today to make the change?

11. Are you an introvert or an extrovert? What challenges and successes have you experienced as a result of that personality trait?

12. This story is written in first person. How would the story be different if it was told from a different perspective such as third person?

13. Charlie and Axyl don't necessarily see a happily-ever-after together. Why do you think the author chose to end the story the way she did?

14. Who was your first crush? Did your story have a happy ending? What did you learn from it?

15. If you could go anywhere on a vacation, where would it be and why?

Understanding Anxiety

It's a normal part of life to experience occasional anxiety. But if you experience anxiety that is persistent, seemingly uncontrollable, and overwhelming, excessive, or irrational, even in everyday situations, it can be disabling. When it interferes with daily activities, you may have an anxiety disorder.

Anxiety disorders (there are three main categories) are the most common and pervasive mental disorders in the United States. Nearly 40 million people in the United States (18%) experience an anxiety disorder in any given year. Approximately 8% of children and teenagers experience an anxiety disorder with most people developing symptoms before age 21.

Researchers are learning that anxiety disorders run in families, like allergies, diabetes, and other disorders. Anxiety disorders may develop from many risk factors that include genetics, brain chemistry, personality, and life events.

Strategies to help you cope
- Take a time-out
- Eat well-balanced meals
- Limit alcohol and caffeine
- Get enough sleep.
- Exercise daily
- Take deep breaths
- Count to 10 slowly
- Do your best, but don't expect perfection
- Accept that you cannot control everything
- Welcome humor
- Maintain a positive attitude
- Get involved
- Learn what triggers your anxiety

- **Talk to someone**
- **Make a list of 10 things you're grateful for**

https://adaa.org/understanding-anxiety

Coming Soon...

If You'd Met Me First
Hearts in Quarantine Series

He'd only ever seen her from a distance. The sidewalk below their building, to be exact. His mind went back to that evening six months ago.

She stood on tiptoe on the sidewalk, even though she was in heels that made her shapely legs look fantastic, craning her neck to see down the street as if looking for someone or something. She checked her phone and then stared down the street in the other direction.

Krew leaned over the balcony railing, glancing up and down the street, too. What was she waiting for? An Uber? A friend? Family? A boyfriend? The city bus stopped farther down the street.

Krew pulled back from the railing so the observer didn't become the observed. The spaces between the railing were wide enough that he could sit back and watch without anyone knowing. He had always been intrigued with people watching. Not in a creepy, peeking-through-windows-and-getting-arrested way. Just a natural curiosity about people, their emotions and interactions with fellow humans inhabiting the same sphere kind of way. Everyone had a story and he liked to see if he could piece it together with the little information he was able to glean through a few minutes of scrutiny. It wasn't nearly enough time to make an accurate picture, he knew, but he was generous when he made up the rest.

And it didn't hurt that the observed today was beautiful. At least that's what he suspected of the woman from this bird's eye view.

Her dress had that never-been-worn-before look to it with precise creases and vivid color. Her blonde hair was up in one of those complicated twists that looked marginally difficult to achieve and

165

majorly uncomfortable. Even so, Krew had to admire the work women went to to impress.

So she was going out. Out with whom?

She looked at her phone again and exhaled a sigh loud enough that he heard it from three stories up. Irritated. Krew wagered it was a late Uber driver and she was going to miss a plane.

Scratch that. No luggage.

She punched a few buttons on her phone and held it up to her ear. Bits of her conversation floated on the autumn breeze up to him.

"...you coming?"

Pause.

She used too informal of a tone for an Uber driver, Krew decided. *Family?*

"...going to call?"

Pause.

Krew watched her pace down the stretch of sidewalk that extended along the length of the building and back. Her heels clacked on the ground, spearing red and yellow leaves unfortunate enough to have fallen in her determined path. Krew tried not to notice how they showed off her legs to their best advantage.

"...understand."

Pause.

Funny, her tone and body language didn't convey her understanding. *Friend who had to cancel suddenly because she had something unexpected pop up?*

"...work that night."

Pause.

Setting something up for another time? Krew wondered. Hm. *Date? Boyfriend?*

"...can't quit my job!"

Unreasonable requests. *Definitely boyfriend. And not a very understanding one from the sound of it.*

"...a good job."

Pause.

"...moving in with you!"

Pause. Weariness covered her shoulders like an expensive wrap. *Had they had this conversation before?*

"...love you too."

Pause. Not the face of a woman in love. Krew frowned, then watched in fascination as the woman stabbed the end button on her phone, cocked back her arm as if to throw said phone, then, thinking better of the action, lowered her arm to her side. With the hand not holding the phone, she swiped at the lingering emotion on her cheeks, squared her shoulders and lifted her chin, and glided into the apartment.

Moments later, Krew heard the door of the apartment next to his open and close. Hm. *My neighbor?* This woman lived right next door and he'd never met her? He was intrigued. Probably far more than he should be considering she had a boyfriend. Maybe.

Three minutes later, Krew heard her door open and close again and the ding of the elevator.

A few minutes after that, Krew saw the woman pull out of the apartment complex in a little green clunker. His brows rose in surprise at the disparity between the way she dressed and carried herself and her unfortunate mode of transportation. She'd be lucky if she made it to where she was going. The thing looked like it was held together with duct tape. He'd wager one of those city street scooters would be more reliable.

Good for you, he still silently cheered her on. *Don't sit around tonight when you look like that! Go out. Show that idiot what he's missing.*

His phone pinged with a text, pulling his thoughts from his beautiful, mysterious neighbor. He dug it out of his pocket.

Briggs: Are you a loser, sitting at home on a Friday night?

Krew shook his head and smiled at his friend's text.

Krew: If UR asking, UR more of a loser than me

Briggs: That hurts

Krew: DYK the people in the apartment next to yours?

Briggs: Random...and no

Briggs: Do you?

Krew: Yes. No. Kindof

Mostly no.

Briggs: RU voyeuring again? Please tell me you're not. DYK the lists you'll be on if you get caught?!

Krew: You make it sound sick and twisted. I call it observing

Briggs: You say Caribbean. I say Caribbean

Krew: It's the same thing, man.

Briggs: You gotta listen to the inflection, bro. Why don't you get a life instead of peeping on others'?

Krew: Says the guy who's txting me from home on a Friday night!

Briggs: Fine. I'm not afraid to admit it. What did you find out about the people next door?

Krew: Stop living vicariously through me

Briggs: I'm coming over. Got any beer in the fridge?

Krew: You know the answer to that. Besides, she left

Briggs: She? It's all becoming a little more clear

Krew: It's not like that. She has a boyfriend

Briggs: Tough break. I'm still coming over

Krew: CU in 10

Want more great reads from Heather?
Visit:https://www.amazon.com/Heather-M.-Green/e/B07CWLNQSR/ref=sr_ntt_srch_lnk_1?qid=1534374442&sr=8-1 **or Facebook.com/localartisancollective/ to purchase her other books in paperback or ebook, and to follow her for updates on new releases.**

Heather would love to hear from you! Follow her on FB or Instagram or send her an email at hgreen534@gmail.com

About the Author

Heather M. Green lives in Utah where it's 'a little bit Country and a little bit Rock 'n' Roll'. She graduated with a Bachelor's degree in Elementary Education with a Special Education emphasis from Weber State University. Heather has one husband, five children, two sons- in- law, one dog, one bird, and one snake. She loves to read, listen to country music, take road trips, spend time at the ocean, and play games with family.

Made in the USA
Columbia, SC
23 June 2023